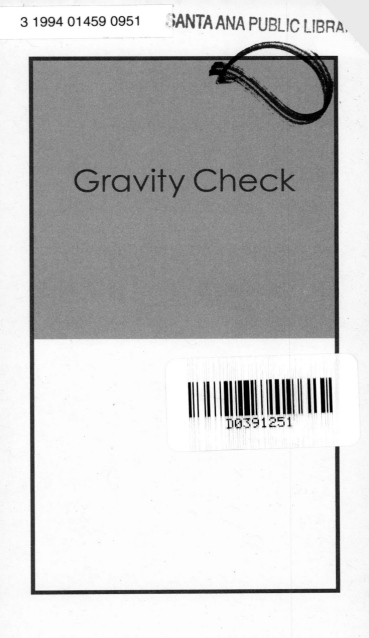

Gravity Check

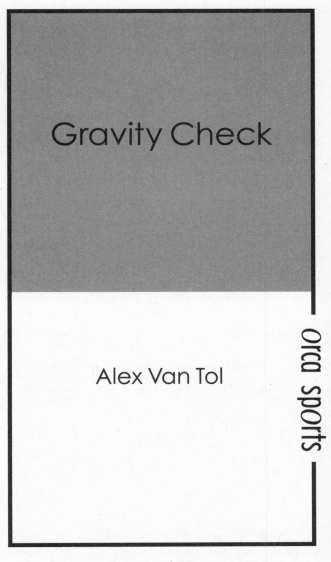

Gravity Check

Alex Van Tol

orca sports

ORCA BOOK PUBLISHERS

Library and Archives Canada Cataloguing in Publication

Van Tol, Alex
Gravity check / Alex Van Tol.
(Orca sports)

Issued also in electronic format.
ISBN 978-1-55469-349-8

I. Title. II. Series: Orca sports
PS8643.A63G73 2011   JC813'.6   C2010-907998-1

First published in the United States, 2011
Library of Congress Control Number: 2010942093

Summary: Jamie and his brother Seth stumble upon a marijuana grow-op
when they go mountain biking in the backcountry.

Mixed Sources
Product group from well-managed forests,
controlled sources and recycled wood or fiber
www.fsc.org Cert no. SW-COC-000952
© 1996 Forest Stewardship Council

*Orca Book Publishers is dedicated to preserving the environment and has printed
this book on paper certified by the Forest Stewardship Council.*

Orca Book Publishers gratefully acknowledges the support for its publishing
programs provided by the following agencies: the Government of Canada
through the Canada Book Fund and the Canada Council for the Arts,
and the Province of British Columbia through the BC Arts Council
and the Book Publishing Tax Credit.

Typesetting by Christine Toller
Cover photography by Getty Images

ORCA BOOK PUBLISHERS
PO Box 5626, Stn. B
Victoria, BC Canada
V8R 6S4

ORCA BOOK PUBLISHERS
PO Box 468
Custer, WA USA
98240-0468

www.orcabook.com
Printed and bound in Canada.

14 13 12 11 • 4 3 2 1

*For Colin, whose support has made my career
as a writer possible.*

chapter one

It's been rainy this year. Every time the forest trails have a chance to dry out a bit, another big dump of H_2O comes along and turns the dirt back into slop.

I don't mind. I'm okay with slop.

I edge along a tricky section of trail, staying high to keep my wheels moving. I don't want to slip down into the mud pit below. It's fun to get muddy, but deep, sucking craters of the stuff tend to slow you down a bit. And gum up your bike.

I'm good for about ten feet. Then my rear tire hits a wet patch and starts to slide. I lean forward and mash the pedals, transferring my weight onto the front tire. I hope it's got some bite.

Yep. Uh...nope. My front tire catches, then spins. I'm finished. I give up and take the slip 'n slide to the bottom.

I come to a stop and find my footing in the deep mud. I pull my bike out from under me. About a pound of black clay decorates my shorts. Another pound has crammed itself into the chain and gearshift.

Out here on the trails, there's nothing I can do about mud in my gears. Some of it will clear out when I start riding again. I'll give my bike a good hose down when we get home. Otherwise the gunk will harden into noisy little grindies that'll mess up my shifting.

I hear a laugh and look up the hill. My little brother Seth is standing at the start of the slippery section. "Nice one, Jamie," he calls. "But let me show you how it's done." Seth grabs his handlebars and prepares to push off.

I doubt he'll make it. Especially since I left him a nice skid track to follow. "You're not going to make it across, Seth," I say. "Not if I came down."

Seth laughs again. "I'm not planning on bogging out, bro."

I feel my ears grow hot. It's not often that I flunk a section, so I'm feeling a bit choked right now. "Just wait a sec, man," I say. "You're not going to make it, so let me get out of your way." I carry my bike a few steps to where the mud isn't so deep and set it down. I swing my leg over the crossbar and crank on the pedals. My tires slip, but then they grab. I squint as mud flings off my front tire. It's a grunt, but a few good pushes haul me out of the hole and onto the forest floor.

Where does Seth get off being so cocky? As if he's actually going to make this section. If I crapped out, then there's a good chance he will too. He hasn't been riding as long as I have.

It burns me that he's so sure of himself. He's always like that. It's like nothing

3

fazes him. But at the same time, I admire him for it. And I envy him for it too.

Which basically makes me hate him.

Everyone I know would be shocked to hear me say that. My teachers, my friends, my grandparents, my swim coach.

Okay, maybe my parents know how I feel. Just a little bit. It's hard to hide stuff, especially from my mom.

I'm pretty sure Mom and Dad have started to piece things together. I think that's why they decided to send us to camp for two weeks. We leave tomorrow morning.

I know what you're thinking. Camp? Sounds kinda hokey. Like we're five and six instead of fifteen and sixteen. But it's not just a camp, you know, like with sing-alongs and Capture the Flag and crafts. It's a biking camp. Mountain biking.

On the slope above me, Seth launches. I watch as his bike goes through the exact motions mine did a couple of minutes ago. Roll. Slip. Grab. Slip. Slow slide to the bottom.

Satisfied, I suppress a grin.

Seth lies in the mud for a moment, staring at the sky. Then he gets to his feet. He looks down at himself. "Wow, man," he says. "I got, like, a mud enema back there."

I can't help it. I laugh.

"I warned you," I say. "But you never listen to me anymore."

"I can make my own decisions, thanks," he snaps. "You don't always have to play big brother." He picks his bike up and carries it out of the mud pit.

His words make me angry, but I decide to let it go. I'd rather keep riding than get into an argument.

I shoulder my bike, and we hoof it back up through the trees to the main trail. Mom's going to love seeing our mud-caked clothes today. Knowing her, she'll make us strip down to our boxers before even letting us inside the house.

We blaze along the path, bumping over roots, catching air on little lifts and slogging through more muddy pitches. Neither of us talks. We just enjoy the feeling of spooling along the trail, soaking up everything in our path.

I love mountain biking. I got into it a couple of years ago, with a cheap hardtail on the dirt track at the park near our place. Naturally, Seth wanted in on the action, so he got a bike too.

I spend a lot of my free time checking out the trails around the fringes of the city. It's a big city. There are a lot of trails, and a lot of them are forested, like this one. Sometimes Seth comes with me. When we're getting along, that is.

And when he's not too busy.

Seth's got a lot of friends. He's Mr. Popularity. He talks so much in class that he doesn't get his work done. So he spends a lot of time playing catch-up at home. Except lately, he's been having more trouble catching up.

I think my parents are hoping this camp is going to be some kind of bonding experience for me and my brother. Something that'll bring us back together. Like we used to be.

Although we're in different grades at school, Seth and I have always done everything together. When we were little, we ate together, napped together, played together. Threw tantrums together. We shared the same room until last year, when our family moved closer to the university and added an extra bedroom to our world.

Seth and I have a lot of the same interests. Mountain biking being one. Basketball, Big Gulps and girls being others. Whenever people see one of us, they always ask where the other one is.

For a long time, I never cared that people talked about me and Seth in the same breath. It's like mac and cheese. You don't think of one without the other.

But lately...I don't know. Seth's been driving me crazy. If I'm honest with myself, it's because I'm jealous of Seth. I'm not as popular. Not as good-looking. Not as funny. Somehow over this past year, when I wasn't paying attention, my little brother became Mr. Big.

On one level, I hate him for it.

But on another, he's still my kid brother. It's a messed-up feeling. I mean, Seth hasn't really done anything to deserve my resentment. It's not like he woke up one morning and said, *Gee, I think I'll be more popular than Jamie today.* But I can't stand him just the same. How he always knows the right thing to say. How everyone loves him, including teachers.

It's sick.

And not in a good way.

chapter two

"You guys hungry?" our camp counselor asks from the head of our table. He cranes his head toward the kitchen. "I think it's pizza for lunch."

"Sounds good to me, Chase," says the skinny kid with glasses. I can't remember his name right now. He sat in the first seat on the bus on the way up. Talked to the driver the entire time. That would make me nuts if I was driving. To have a know-it-all kid squawking in my ear for an hour and a half? No thanks. The driver didn't seem to mind though.

The bus dropped us off with our bags and bikes about an hour ago. You should have heard everyone grumbling about leaving our iPods and cell phones at home for two whole weeks.

You have to admit, it *is* a bit of a drag.

For me, though, it's a worthwhile exchange. I want to be here. I'm looking forward to two straight weeks of bumps, jumps and awesome downhills.

I look around the lodge. It's busy, noisy, full of people moving around. And it smells great. My stomach rumbles, and I realize how hungry I am.

I look back at Chase. He seems like a laid-back kind of guy. Big and muscular, like he could bulldoze you in a heartbeat. He's sunburned, and his hair is a wild tangle of curls, but he's got a nice face. Friendly. Early twenties. He told us this is his sixth year of being a counselor at Camp Edgelow. Six, man! He must have started when he was my age or something. I wonder if maybe he goes to the university where my dad teaches.

Chase is hollering along with a noisy camp cheer now, pounding on the table as the program staff prepare to make their after-lunch announcements. Sitting next to Chase is the skinny kid from the bus. I remember his name now. Nolan. What a perfect name. He's exactly how you'd picture a Nolan. Sharp, alert expression, like a raccoon. Skinny. Smudgy glasses. Hair that sticks up in the back. He's obviously a total nerd. I wonder what he's doing here, in an intermediate mountain-biking group. He's the kind of kid that other kids would make life hard for in school. Not that I would. I'm not a dick like that. I don't need to make other people feel bad to make myself feel better.

Seth's sitting next to Nolan, but let's just skip over his blond, blue-eyed, grinning, freckled perfection and move on to the last person in our small group.

Rico. He's our junior counselor. From what I can tell, he's the strong, silent type. He seems cool. Doesn't talk unless he needs to say something. Not like Chase and Nolan, who are both motormouths.

Seth's a talker too. The three of them will get on famously, I'll bet.

Whatever. I'm going to focus on having fun this week, not on how Seth drives me crazy.

As of tomorrow morning, our group is headed off-site for four days of pure mountain-biking excitement. Chase says when we're done lunch, we'll need to figure out our menus and pack our gear. We'll still be able to get a couple hours of biking in before supper too. I'm a bit bummed that we're not going to be sticking around to explore all the terrain around here. But I'm sure there'll be even crazier tracks where we're headed. First thing tomorrow, we'll load our bikes onto a trailer and take the van up into the hills. Deep into the mountains. Where I can ditch my worries on the rolling single track.

Just me, my bike and my wits, duking it out with the dirt trails.

And my baby brother Seth far, far behind me.

Sweet.

chapter three

Chase says there's a pump track here, and we can go there after we've packed for our overnight! *Awesome*. I had no idea the camp had one. They're superhard to build and a lot of places don't even allow them. I guess I shouldn't be that surprised. I mean, this *is* a mountain-biking camp, after all.

I've never been on a full-fledged pump track before. I've just played around on the jumps that Seth and I have built up in the woods near our place. I'm totally busting to try it.

After we finish packing, we hop on our bikes and pedal down to the pump track. I love my bike. Last year, I was riding hard-tail on an old Hahanna from, like, the Ice Age. But by April, I'd finally saved enough to buy my Kona Cadabra. It's the sweetest ride. It's more work to pedal this sucker uphill, because the suspension adds weight. But the ride down is way, way finer. Pumping and jumping is a snap on this bounce machine.

Seth's got my old bike. It'll be good to him. He'll have to save up for another one, though, if he wants a better ride. As if that'll happen. Seth burns through money like a welding torch through pipe. Doesn't matter how many hours he works at the sub shop, he spends his paychecks as soon as they come in.

Nolan, Chase, Seth and Rico follow a short gravel road that leads straight down from the out-tripping building. I spot a path in the trees and take that instead. I didn't sign up for road biking!

The trail is short, dry, narrow and packed with roots. Primo. It's not a steep slope, so I don't even try to avoid the bumps. I stand on the pedals and rattle straight over them. I eat bumps for breakfast. I savor the jerky motion that the path creates in my wrists. My bike feels great. Tight and compact. Like an extension of my body.

I arrive at the bottom of the hill, primed and ready for more. I follow the others, cutting through a field of long grass. On the other side of a small hill, a huge oval has been carved up into paths. It's about the size of an Olympic swimming pool. Maybe bigger. And it's filled—jammed, criss-crossed—with waves, berms and jumps. My mouth waters just looking at it.

The pump track.

"Whoa," Seth says. His eyes are huge in his face. "This is the dopest pump track *ever.*" I roll my eyes. Like he would know. How many pump tracks has he been on? Exactly none.

Nolan nods sagely. He looks like a skinny version of Harry Potter, without the scar.

Chase steps off his bike and turns to us. "Welcome to the Camp Edgelow pump track, guys. I'll give you a quick rundown of the rules. Skid lids, always. No rule about pads or guards here, but I'd never stop you from wearing protective gear. Only one guy at a time on the track. And stay in control. Okay?" He looks out at the pump track. I can tell he's pretty excited too. "Watch me." And he takes off.

It's a total stoke watching him ride. My heart races, and my eyes feast on his every move. I can practically feel the adrenaline spurting into my bloodstream every time he flips off a lip and catches air. Up, down, up, around, down. Every motion Chase makes is as smooth and fluid as a surfer riding a mother wave. He's got it dialed. The guy's incredible!

Chase rides around the pump track a couple of times. He pulls out some fancy freestyle moves just to show off. He doesn't spin the pedals around once. That's the whole idea of a pump track—to get all the way around by using only the movement of your body and your bike.

Seth and Nolan cheer as Chase skids to a stop in a puff of dust. I dish the applause too, a huge grin splitting my face.

"How about it?" Chase asks, breathing hard. Seth hoots, and we all nod. "Few pointers before you head out," Chase says. "The goal here is to get you pumping so you can have better traction and more control. It's a pump track, right? PUMP track."

I nod, but Seth asks, "Better traction and more control? Doesn't that translate into *going slower*?"

Chase shakes his head. "Actually, it's the opposite. If you keep your body fluid, you can use the transitions and rollers to go faster. Think of a mogul skier whose legs move like pistons. Or a surfer soaking up wave chop with his legs. His upper body is quiet, right? Not moving a lot." We're all listening intently, so Chase continues. "Same thing on the pump track. You use your arms and legs to add or decrease pressure on the wheels. The traction lets you store up energy to get over the next obstacle.

17

You'll actually end up moving faster by applying pressure to the track at the right times. And," he adds, "you'll be in control. Which is the most important thing."

The physics of it makes sense to me, but it's too much for Nolan to take in. "Hold it," he says. "Can you go over that again, Chase?" I half expect him to whip out a pad and pencil and start taking notes.

"I'll do you one better," Chase replies. "I'll go around again. This time, watch how I stay active on the bike. Moving forward and back as well as up and down."

He pushes off again and rides another smooth circuit. I think about what he said about the skier's legs sucking up the moguls. I can hear the knobs on his tires gripping as he corners, deep and swooping, in front of us and heads back into the bowl for the jumps across the center.

"That's wicked," Seth says as Chase hits a jump, gobbles air and tracks smoothly down the backside.

"I don't know, you guys," says Nolan. He takes his glasses off and rubs the lenses on the corner of his T-shirt. When he puts them back on, he sighs. "It looks pretty technical to me."

"It can be as technical as you want," I point out. "Or not. You don't have to go as fast as Chase. You're not supposed to be pro, Nolan. You're here to learn. Just go however fast feels safe. They're jumps for him," I say, jerking my thumb in Chase's direction, "but they can be bumps for you."

Rico chimes in, and we all turn to look. He hasn't said much of anything all day. "Your speed determines the nature of the obstacle," he says to Nolan. "You don't have to burn it up on your first go-around."

Nolan considers this. "Yeah, you're right," he agrees. "No burning on the first round."

Chase swoops in again, braking to a stop in front of our little group. "Who's up?" he says with a grin.

chapter four

Seth jumps up, punching his fist into the air like a kindergarten kid who Knows The Answer.

"Me!" Seth yells. "I'm going!"

I let Seth have his moment. I can wait. I mean, I can *hardly* wait. But I can wait.

Nolan isn't about to argue with Seth. In fact, Nolan looks like he might pee his pants right about now. He's so not ready. I want to laugh, but I don't.

I watch Seth drop in and go around the track once, pedaling lightly as he gets a feel for the obstacles and transitions. Twice around, this time a bit faster. He leans into a curve, pushing his wheels hard against the side of a berm.

"Right on, Seth!" Chase shouts. "That's the way." Seth grins and speeds up a bit, pulling up on the handlebars and pushing down on his pedals as he negotiates the bumps. He gets a good head of steam up and catches big air off the lip of a bump. Showoff. He's rushing into it.

He pulls up on his handlebars too hard, raising the bike's nose.

Beside me, Nolan whoops, then gasps as Seth comes down. His back tire hits hard, followed by his front wheel. Both feet come off the pedals, and he drags heavy to keep his balance. I can see he's scared, but he has the sense not to lock his wheels.

I gotta hand it to him. He ends a stupid stunt with a clean recovery.

Typical.

"Yeah, remember that bit I mentioned about staying in control, Seth?" yells Chase. We all laugh.

Seth does another lap, nice and tight this time. He rolls to a stop at the top of the berm we're standing on. His wide smile tells me how much he likes the pump track. I know, like me, he's already making plans for one in our neighborhood.

"Dude! That was supreme!" Seth shouts. "I want to go again!"

"All in good time, Seth." Chase smiles. "Everybody gets a turn." He looks around at me, Rico and Nolan.

Nolan sticks up his hands, palms out, and shakes his head. "You go, Rico," he says. "I'll watch you."

I let Rico step forward. He's pretty experienced, being a junior counselor and all. Besides, I'll get a better picture of the terrain by watching the other guys ride it ahead of me.

Rico rolls his bike smoothly into the pit. He rides nice. Slow but fluid, like a snake through water. We watch and listen as Chase points out Rico's form and technique. Rico is completely focused, fully in the moment. He's good.

He does three laps. He lets himself pop up off the last few jumps. Does a couple little handlebar twists. Then he wheels in.

I look at Nolan and raise my eyebrows. He nods and steps forward. He rides two laps, pedaling much of the way, but he's got the pumping action pretty good. Not bad at all.

"Nice work, Nolan!" Seth shouts. Rico and Chase whistle. When Nolan gets back to the group, his eyes are shining behind his glasses. He seems to have grown taller somehow.

I drop in while they're still patting him on the back. He talks excitedly about his ride. He'll be yapping about it for another two hours, I bet.

I take off, coasting down the first slope. Up onto a bump, back down into a valley. I ride several more waves, easy and loose. Around a curve. I pedal across a berm, looking ahead and scanning the terrain on my first time around. I won't be pedaling for long. Soon I'll be using only my weight and pumping action to move the bike across the ground. Swooping low around corners. Pulling up and pushing down, riding the waves, over and over. It's the same motion you see horse jumpers using when they're leaping over high rails and water traps.

Same principle. Except this ride goes faster and involves a lot more dirt.

As I think about the motions—up, down, pull, push, pump—my body follows. My attention narrows, focusing to a sharp point. I pick up speed, and everything to the side of the track falls away. I don't see anything but the rolling dirt path ahead. I keep my head up, scanning the track, planning my route. Riding it hard. Active. I shoot across a series of waves, gaining speed with each drop. I'm a pogo stick on wheels. My legs and arms act separately, like shock absorbers.

I pump harder on the second round, dropping my shoulders and pressing into the transitions to build my speed. I become one with my bike. And we become one with the track, a marble rolling fast along a narrow chute.

I swoop into a berm, keeping my butt low in the saddle and pushing my rear tire into the wall. I shoot out of it and over a hump, catching air and coming down clean on both tires. With traction. In control.

Fast.

Then another series of bumps. Up. Off. Air. Down. Up. Off. Air.

Again.

A chorus of cheers erupts from the other end of the pump track, and I finish my last lap with a huge grin. Chase claps my back. Nolan claps his hands. Seth matches my grin, and Rico high-fives me.

Bike camp rocks.

chapter five

Sunlight wakes me up, streaming through the cobwebby window beside my bed. I struggle into a sitting position. My sleeping bag gapes open, and a blast of cold air hits my arms. Holy crap, is it ever cold in here! It's gotta be minus five. It's colder in this cabin than it is outside, I'm sure of it. I gather my bag around my neck, closing it off so my body stays warm.

Chase is already gone from his bunk. How did he leave without waking any of us?

I can see Nolan's head poking out of his sleeping bag. He's peering around with bright eyes. Probably calculating the factor by which his body's molecules are slowed in subzero temperatures.

Rico's still conked out, facing the wall. His side moves slowly with his breathing. Up, down. Up, down. He's not waking up anytime soon.

Seth sits up, and I look over. He grins, and I smile back. I always feel good in the morning. Just as Seth is slipping his shoes on to head to the outhouse, Chase bursts through the door.

"Up and at 'em, guys. It's seven twenty. Didn't you hear the wake-up bell?" He looks around at our groggy forms, his eyes coming to rest on his junior counselor. "I'm guessing not."

Seth grimaces as he pulls on his shoes. I can imagine how cold they feel. I wiggle my toes inside my warm sleeping bag and yawn.

Chase looks at Seth. "Good," he says. "You're ready. You can come help set the breakfast table."

Seth shakes his head. "Not me, man. I gotta whiz. Take Jamie." He slips past Chase and out into the cold morning air.

Chase looks at me. "How fast can you be ready?" he asks.

I groan. "Not as fast as Nolan," I say. Couldn't Chase pick on someone small for the first job of the day?

Nolan stops cleaning his glasses to give me the finger. I laugh. The kid's all right.

"You have five minutes," Chase tells me. "Meet you up at the lodge." He gives Rico a not-too-gentle nudge with his foot. "Awaken, co-counselor. There are children to lead."

Rico groans, and Chase grins. He ducks out, the door slamming behind him.

I grunt and swing my legs, still inside my sleeping bag, over the side of my bunk. I pick my jeans up off the floor, where I dropped them last night. They're freezing. Oh, man. How am I supposed to put these on? But the alternative—wearing my boxers to breakfast—isn't very appealing. So I slide my legs in, gritting my teeth to stop them from chattering.

"You should sleep with them."

I look over at Nolan.

"Pardon?" I say. It comes out sounding really snarly. But I'm feeling kind of snarly, having to cram my toasty lower half into what feels like a bag of shaved ice.

"Sleep with your jeans, I said. You won't even notice them in the bottom of your sleeping bag," Nolan says. "And then you don't have to get into cold clothes in the morning."

I grunt again. It's a good idea, but I'm not about to give him the satisfaction of hearing it. I slip a shirt over my head and slide my feet into my Vans. My morning cheeriness has evaporated. Now I have to take a leak too. I wriggle into my fleece jacket, then step outside.

Once I'm there, things start to look better. It's freezing, yeah, but the sky is a clear blue. It'll warm up.

Today's the day they take us up into the hills and drop us off to ride.

For four days straight. No wake-up bells, no tables to set, no time wasted. Just miles and miles of empty forest, and beautiful trails waiting to be devoured.

At the drop-off point, we pull our bikes off the trailer. From here, the van driver will head to the campsite and drop off our packs. We'll explore the trails a bit as we head toward the overnight spot.

We've only got our hydration packs with us. Food, water, repair stuff. Rico has one first-aid kit, Chase has the other. Chase also has a satellite phone from the camp. The senior counselors are required to have their sat phones with them at all times.

We get set up and check our bikes over. All systems go.

Rico rustles around inside a plastic bag and pops a handful of trail mix into his mouth. My stomach grumbles. I realize I'm hungry again, even though it's only been a couple of hours. I look around at the sun's position in the sky. I bet it's after ten already.

Nolan's got a watch. Of course.

"Yo, No," I say. "What time is it?"

Nolan shoves aside the strap of his biking glove and peers at his wrist. His glasses slide down his nose. He slides them back up with his other wrist. I watch as the strap on his glove slips back down and covers his watch again. He shoves it out of the way and holds it with his other hand. He loses his grip on his bag of trail mix. It falls from his hand, but he sticks his foot out and catches it before it hits the ground. It's a weird, comical mix of clumsy and graceful. "It's ten seventeen," he announces.

"Man, no wonder I'm starving," says Seth. He unzips his bag and pulls out his own stash of trail mix. Everybody else likes the idea, and pretty soon we're all sitting around on the grass, scarfing peanuts, raisins and M&M's and listening to Chase tell us about some of the crashes he's witnessed over the years.

"Here's what you've got to remember, boys," he says with a grin. He's got us peeing our pants laughing about the guy who jetted off a boulder and did a face-plant into a pile of deer turds. "Your brakes don't work in midair. Doesn't matter how hard you squeeze 'em. But keep the rubber *down*, now." He nods. "You'll be all right."

He waits until the last of our laughter dies away and we're all sitting forward, waiting to hear his next story. Suddenly he's all business. "I've got some news for you guys. Tomorrow, we're going to be joined for the day by Mitch Woodgrove."

My jaw drops. "Mitch Woodgrove?"

"*The* Mitch Woodgrove?" Nolan squeaks. Chase nods.

"As in, *Canadian freeride biking champion* Mitch Woodgrove?" says Seth.

Another nod.

"No way!" Nolan hollers. "No freaking *way*!"

"How did you swing that?" Rico wants to know. "That's the first I've heard of it. Did the program staff arrange it as a surprise?" He's lying on his back, head propped on his water bag, hands linked behind his head.

Chase shakes his head. "Nah. He's a friend of a friend. I met him at a party a couple of months ago. I asked whether he'd come to camp one day and share some tips for handling jumps and bumpy terrain. Ordered him up special just for you guys."

"Right on," I say. "Thanks, Chase." I tie the top of my trail-mix bag into a knot and stuff it back in my bag. "That's definitely something to look forward to."

"Should be," says Chase. "They don't come much better than Mitch. And he was only too happy to come all the way up here, which kind of surprised me. But I guess he's pretty keen on sharing his expertise with younger riders."

"Wow," says Nolan. "I can't believe we're going to get to meet Mitch Woodgrove. That's just the coolest thing ever."

"Uh, correction," says Rico. "That'd be me. Mitch Woodgrove is the second-coolest thing ever."

We laugh, and Chase gets to his feet. "All right, boys. Tea party's over. We came here to ride. Let's get at it!"

chapter six

The hardpack under my tires feels great as we hammer off into the bush. Every so often, there's a little section that climbs or drops through the trees. We have fun with it, whooping and shouting as we hammer over the little bumps, looking for air anywhere we can.

It's a beautiful day, and I'm so stoked that Mitch is coming that my issues with Seth have taken a backseat. I dip my head down and peek under my arm. Seth's right behind me. He's having a good time too. He sees me and grins, pushing hard off his pedals and exploding his bike straight up into the air. Bunny hop! He hoots when I give him one in return.

Things are definitely okay between us today.

After a particularly jangly section of roots, we come to the lip of a stairlike spread of rock that heads downhill. It's weird how nature comes up with this stuff. The pitch looks exciting. But I've never run a long flight of stairs before. And these ones are all different lengths and heights. It's pretty technical. I wonder how Nolan will handle it.

We're all feeling pretty tapped out after that last section. But it's not far to our campsite now, so we decide to keep going instead of stopping for a rest. Chase gives me the okay to go ahead and scout the rock stairs before the others come down.

I push off the lip and bump down, keeping my weight far back on the seat and riding easy on my brakes. It's a challenging section, not like any stairs I've ever done. I have to be on my game the whole way down, thinking and staying loose on the pedals. I'm careful to only use the littlest bit of pressure on my front brakes. If I squeeze too hard, my front tire will stop dead—and my downward momentum will flip my bike over my head. I rely on my rear brakes instead.

At the bottom, I ease to a stop and move my bike off the path.

That was good fun. I decide that when everyone's down, I'll go back up and do it a few more times.

I turn and give the thumbs up to Rico, who rides down next. Smooth as a slinky, that guy. He gives me a grin when he's down. I think maybe I'll talk to him later about being a junior counselor. Maybe I can do the same thing next summer.

Nolan's next. He's been watching Rico and me carefully. I can hear Chase up top, reminding him to stay loose and use his rear brakes. Then Nolan's off, wobbling a bit. Just when I think maybe he should get off and walk, he drops onto the first stair. No stopping him now.

Boy, was that ever right. There's no stopping Nolan at all.

He plunges over the first few steps, then gets freaked out and tries to rein it in.

I watch as he hits his front brakes. Rico sees the same thing.

"Nolan!" he shouts. "Off your front brakes!" But it's too late. Nolan's into the spill. There's no going back. My heart leaps into my mouth as I watch his back end tip up, up, up and over. Then he's falling, end over end, stuff flying out of his pack, bumping and smashing down the whole mess of steps. With every revolution, he gains speed.

At last, he reaches the bottom of the stairs and crashes to a stop. His bike lands on top of him. It looks bad. The universe suddenly shifts into slow motion when Nolan stops moving. No one says anything for a second. Even the birds are quiet. The bike's rear wheel spins gently in the still air.

From the top of the stairs, I can hear Seth's voice drifting to me. "Holy crap, man. That was a wicked endo. Is he okay?"

I look up. From the expression on Chase's face, I can tell he's thinking it's going to be ugly. Nolan might have broken his neck.

Time speeds up again, and I take a gulp of air.

Rico and I drop our bikes and run to where Nolan is lying all crumpled and bent under the frame of his bike. Gear fans out around where he landed. His water bottle. His sunscreen. His glasses (not broken, thankfully). Lip balm. Trail mix. A map. A package of Kleenex perches in a tree nearby, like some random passerby found it on the trail and put it there for easy spotting.

From above, Chase shouts at me. "Don't move him, Jamie!" He launches himself down the stepped rock slope on foot, slinging off his pack, his hands fumbling with the zipper of the first-aid kit before he even comes to a stop at the bottom. Seth follows, taking the stairs in big leaps.

"He might have a spinal," Rico says to me. He's breathing hard. I am too.

Jesus. A spinal? Out here?

"Nolan, can you hear me?" Chase says, his voice louder than usual.

Nolan's voice is muffled, but it's there. "I can hear you fine, Chase. You don't have to shout." My heart drops out of my mouth and back into my chest and starts beating again. Chase looks at me. There's relief in the little smile on his face. Nolan's not dead. And he probably hasn't broken his neck, either.

As if to answer my thoughts, Nolan waves his arms weakly. "Hello? Can somebody please get this bike off me?"

"Sure, yeah." Chase gives me the nod, and we gingerly lift the bike off Nolan. When we've got the bike untangled from his legs and pack straps, he rolls himself into a sitting position and gives his head a shake. Dust puffs off his helmet. Rico gives him a careful once-over. Nolan's knees are bleeding pretty good, his chin is a red meaty mess, and he's got big strips of skin missing from each forearm. I wince when I see them. So does Nolan. Those are going to hurt. He stares at his bleeding wounds and takes a big, shaky breath. I wonder whether we're going to have to take him back to camp. A wipeout like that is enough to strike fear into the heart of any cyclist. And we've got four full days out here. I doubt whether he's going to want to keep going.

Everyone is silent, staring at him, watching to see how he's going to manage his first serious stack.

Nolan looks around at the mess spread around on the ground nearby. He takes another shaky breath.

"Wow," he says. He looks up at Rico and blinks. Then he looks back at the gear that's strewn everywhere. "Holy. Got me quite the yard sale, here, eh?"

Seth and I burst out laughing.

Chase grins. "Let's get you patched up, Nolan," he says. He rummages in his first-aid kit.

And just like that, we're back in business.

chapter seven

The rest of the day passes in a blur of biking. No more serious bails, though, thank god. Chase did a good job of dressing Nolan's knees and wrapping his arms. His chin looked a lot better too, after it was cleaned off and all the little bits of gravel were washed out.

By the time we reach the campsite, it's late afternoon. We find our packs tossed in a careless heap, baking in the afternoon sun. I wish a band of gnomes would come set up our tents and make supper for us.

My butt is sore as I dismount and lean my bike on a tree near the fire pit.

I'm not the only one. We're all stiff.

"Augh!" moans Seth as he peels himself off his saddle. "My ass is *so* done with being on that seat."

"Wait until tomorrow morning," says Chase. "You'll be even more sore. Sorer? Is that a word?" He shrugs, shoulders his pack and walks it over to a flat patch of gravel. He looks around the area. "What do you guys say we set the tents up here?"

"You mean, what do we say to *you* setting up the tents for us?" says Seth with a grin. "Sounds good to me. Right where you are looks like a perfect spot, Chase." Seth wanders over to the tree stumps circling the fire pit and eases himself down next to Nolan, who's popping sunflower seeds like they're Smarties. Seth holds out his hand, and Nolan dumps a handful of seeds into his palm.

Chase laughs at Seth's words, and I feel that familiar stab of jealousy. It's always so easy for Seth. He even gets away with being a lazy bum because he's such a charmer. But Chase surprises me with what he says next.

"Not likely," Chase replies. "Sore ass or not, there's work to be done. Rico and Nolan, you two are on supper detail. Jamie and Seth, you're helping me set up the tents. We'll do the bear hang after."

I groan.

"But I just sat down!" Seth whines. Chase ignores him.

Nolan dives headfirst into the bag of food we packed earlier. Rico pumps up the propane stove. Pots rattle and crash as they get to work.

Chase pulls a bundle of poles out of the tent bag. "When you guys get done helping me set up these tents," he says, "I'll give you some free time to roam as long as you're back in time for supper. Tomorrow night we'll switch. You'll be on supper prep and the other guys can have freebies."

"Can we take our bikes?" I ask.

"If you're responsible about it," Chase says, straightening the poles. He looks at us meaningfully.

Seth and I look at each other. Right on! Time to ourselves on the trails? Sweet. My butt feels much less sore as I think about the prospect.

We work like machines, laying down ground sheets, pushing tent poles through sleeves and pounding in pegs. Before long, we've got two nice sleeping shelters set up.

Chase unzips the door to one of the tents and unrolls his sleeping pad. He waits until it inflates, then eases himself down on it. A copy of *Surfer's Path* appears from inside his pack. "Where are you guys headed?" he asks. "It's pretty remote out here. I've got to know where you'll be in case we need to send the search party after you." He winks and nods in the direction of Nolan and Rico.

Nolan's bent over a pot lid, chopping green pepper into little bitty pieces with his Swiss Army knife. His mouth moves as he works. Probably reciting Shakespeare or something. Rico fills the cooking pot, using filtered water from the stream that runs along our campsite. My stomach growls again. I look at the sky. The sun is lowering itself toward the mountains. If Seth and I head out now, we can get a good hour's worth of riding in before we have to pack it in for the night.

"How long until supper, Nolan?" I call.

Nolan stops chopping. He straightens up and wipes his brow with his gauzy arm bandage, like he's just chopped a cord of wood. "Forty-five?" he says.

Good enough.

"You know that trail we saw as we came into camp?" I ask Chase. "The one that heads east through the clearing? We'll take that one."

"Sounds good. But stay on the main trail," he says. "No funny stuff. No jumps, no tricks. You're just exploring now, right?"

"Right. That's fair," I say. "We'll be back for supper."

"Sounds good." Chase returns to his magazine. "Take a first-aid kit with you."

"Check." Seth and I both completed the mandatory first-aid training before we arrived at camp.

Seth is already buckling his helmet. I grab my own helmet and bike, wrestling my hands into gloves that are still damp from a day of sweating. Then we blast.

I know we promised Chase no funny stuff. But come on. How can you tell two bikers to go check out unexplored trails and not mess around while they're doing it?

A few minutes away from the campsite, the trail starts swooping. It's beautiful. Dips and hollows that remind me of the pump track back at camp. A couple of sweet jumps. We backtrack a few times to see how fast we can take them. I'm pleased to discover that I'm getting pretty good at moving my bike around under me when I've caught some good air. A couple of shaky landings, but nothing too ugly.

When we get bored with that, we continue exploring. Seth takes the lead. After a few minutes of going dead straight, Seth pulls off the main track onto a winding side trail that drifts closer to the trees. I like this one already. I'm too excited at seeing rocks and roots to give Seth hell for leaving the main path. After all, I want to have some fun too. We'll just play for a while, I think. Then we'll return to the main trail.

Dodging boulders and hopping roots slows us down a bit. Gradually, the obstacles fade and the trail changes again. The path opens out into an overgrown double track—the kind ATVs use. I'm disappointed. The surrounding forest gets deeper and darker. We ride along the track for a while, looking for a different path into the trees. Or at least for something exciting to jump. Nothing. Just grass and trees flashing past.

I'm about to suggest we turn back when Seth pulls up short. I nearly crash into him. I jerk my front wheel away from his rear tire and hop my bike into the tall weeds growing beside the track. I lose my balance and fall off.

"Jesus, Seth!" I shout. "What's with the roost?" He knows better than to stop dead like that. It's dangerous. If there were other people riding behind us, it'd cause a huge pileup. People get hurt doing that kind of stuff.

He ignores my question.

"You can't just stop like that," I bark. "You're lucky I didn't eat your back fender." I stand and brush myself off, then grab my bike. "Dumbass," I mutter.

"Jamie, look around," Seth says quietly. The way he says it gives me the chills. Immediately, my anger vanishes. I follow his gaze.

For as far as I can see, in every direction, we are surrounded by tall stalks of leafy dark green plants. They're interspersed with the huge coniferous trees in the forest. Blending in.

My jaw drops. "Holy crap," I breathe. "Is that what I think it is?"

Seth nods. "BC Bud. Acres and acres of it." He leans forward and grabs one of the plants. "Just about ready to be harvested too," he says. He looks at me, a mixture of daring and delight in his face. "Perfecto."

"Seth!" I hiss. I grab his hand away from the plant. "Don't even think about it. This stuff doesn't just grow out here naturally. Someone's planted it on purpose. Someone who probably doesn't want a couple of kids helping themselves to their crop," I add. I look around. "Someone who most likely wouldn't want those same kids to even *know* about it."

Suddenly I feel scared. It hits me that we've ridden into a very serious situation. I look around again, craning my neck in all directions. There must be thousands of plants out here. Maybe hundreds of thousands. All mixed in with the surrounding pines.

We're not just on a mountain-biking trail deep in the North Shore Mountains right now.

We're in the middle of a huge grow-op.

I turn to Seth and lower my voice. "This isn't some backwoods hick's little pot patch," I say. "This is a massive grow, man. I bet it's guarded. We have to get out of here. We can't get caught. If they catch us, they'll kill us." I'm not sure if that's exactly true. But...what if it is?

Seth's blue eyes widen. Fear flickers in their depths. He hasn't thought of this. He nods. "Okay," he whispers. "Let's go."

We turn and walk our bikes back the way we came, hardly daring to as much as crinkle the grass under our feet. For some reason that we don't need to discuss, both of us feel better walking rather than biking right now. It feels less noisy. The less attention we draw to ourselves right now, the better.

My chest is tight, like someone has wrapped it in thick rubber bands. We walk for what feels like ages, stopping and goggling at each other in terror whenever one of us snaps a twig or we hear a noise in the forest.

We're almost running by the time we get off the double track. It's not until we're deep onto the single track that we allow ourselves to mount up and ride.

And ride we do. Legs burning, we hammer down the path toward camp, thanking the universe that no one spotted us.

After a few minutes, the forest opens up and we pass the jumps we were playing on earlier. We slacken our pace. Just before we roll into camp, I slow my bike to a stop.

I want to debrief with Seth before we arrive back at the fire pit. We have to figure out what to tell everyone. Or what not to tell.

Seth rolls up beside me. "That was crazy, man," he says. "What the hell? I almost filled my pants back there."

I nod. "Yeah, not fun." I wipe sweat from under my helmet with the side of my glove. "So listen," I say. "We're not going to breathe a word about this to anyone, okay?"

"What?" Seth asks. "Why not?"

"If Chase finds out where we've been, he'll freak."

"Jamie, we just rode our bikes into a major grow-op," says Seth. "I have to tell everyone what happened!"

Of course he does. Seth always wants to be the first one to spread news. But I can't let him. Not this time.

I shake my head. "Listen to me, Seth. If we tell them what we just saw, Chase might make us pack up and leave."

"*What*?" Seth says. "No way. Jamie, the grow-op is at least two miles away from the campsite. It's totally far into the trees," he says, gesturing toward where we've just come from. "No one's going to come chasing after us. If they haven't already, they're not about to."

"I know that," I say. "And you know that. *I* think we're fine too. No one's going to come after us. But Chase and Rico have a job to do. They're supposed to keep us safe. And that means they might call the van to take us back to camp right away." I pause to let this sink in. "And then we might not get to meet Mitch Woodgrove tomorrow."

A light goes on. "Oh," says Seth. "Yeah." He nods slowly as he works it all out in his brain. "Yeah, that would suck."

"Exactly," I say. "So. We're not telling anyone what we saw. And to stop anyone else from going down that same path tomorrow, we'll just say that the terrain was really lame and flat and there was nothing to do. Deal?"

Seth nods. "Yeah, that's good," he says. "They'll buy that."

I look right at him. "Can I trust you not to tell anyone about this, Seth?" I ask. "You have to promise to keep your mouth shut."

Seth nods. "No problem, man," he says. He presses his lips together. Uses his fingers to mime a little locking motion and then throws away an imaginary key.

I nod. "Good."

Our dirty little secret parked firmly in the closet, we hop on our bikes and pedal back to the campsite.

chapter eight

The next morning comes before any of us are ready for it. The air is cold, and we pull our sleeves down over our hands while we wait for the water to boil. The sound of wheels crunching on gravel makes me turn. A tall, broad-shouldered guy pulls up to the fire pit and dismounts from his bike. Mitch Woodgrove. He's bigger than I expected. "Morning, everyone," he says with a wide grin.

"Hey, Mitch!" Chase says. He's standing by the stove, preparing our breakfast.

He extends his hand, and they shake, firm and quick. We nod and wave as Chase introduces us.

"You guys ready to shred?" Mitch asks.

"Hellz yeah!" shouts Seth. His enthusiasm makes me smile.

"For sure," says Rico.

I steal a glance at Nolan, who was so excited last night about Mitch coming that he wouldn't shut up about it. But now the words fail him. He's just staring, slack-jawed and starstruck. I don't even think he heard Mitch's question. I nudge him with my elbow, and he closes his mouth.

"Totally ready, Mitch," I say.

Eight thirty finds us standing with Mitch at the top of a sharp drop in the forest, where we've come to play.

Rico rubs his eyes and yawns. I don't know how the guy can be so tired all the time. I'm wide awake. I don't want to miss a thing today.

"Okay, so you want to be looking ahead," Mitch is saying. "You don't want to be looking down at what your bike is doing.

Look at where you're going to be landing. Concentrate on making yourself go there."

The sun streams through the canopy high above us, lighting up the little plumes of dust kicked up by our wheels. Spread out before us is a whole series of jumps and drops that passing bikers have carved out of the earth over time. It's a mountain-bike playground, deep in the backcountry.

Nolan shifts uneasily next to me as he listens to Mitch. I can see this is taking him pretty far from his comfort zone.

On my other side, Seth is watching Mitch's every move with rapt attention. He's been pissing me off all morning, sucking up to Mitch and trying to make him laugh. So far he hasn't succeeded.

Mitch backs his bike up a bit and hops on. "Have a look, guys." He starts rolling toward the drop, talking all the way. "Make sure your speed is right, lean back, stay loose"—he flies over the lip, and then his wheels hit the hardpack—"and ride it out."

I nod. It's pretty basic technique. Nice to hear Mitch talk us through it though.

I look at Nolan. "What do you say, Nolan?" I ask. "You up for it?"

Nolan shakes his head. "This one's all yours, Jamie," he says. "I'm happy to watch." He must still be really sore from yesterday's fall down those stairs.

"You're coming down too, Nolan," says Mitch from where he's standing at the bottom of the jump. His words are teasing, but his tone is firm.

"We'll see about that," Nolan replies. He crosses his arms like a pouty two-year-old. "You're not the boss of me!"

I laugh at Nolan's act. I know he'll eventually cave and come down the drop. He just has to get used to the idea. Map it out in his mind. Nolan can't stand not being a part of things, even if he sometimes gets in way over his head.

I wheel my bike back from where I've been watching, on the side of the lip. As I turn to start walking it uphill, Chase comes screaming down from another jump higher up on the track. He's got some serious speed—and a serious grin on his face.

"Don't try this at home, kids," he shouts as he launches off the lip. My eyes nearly fall out of my head as I watch him chew through the air. He drops his bike down, below his body. Swings his legs forward. Slaps the soles of his feet together. Whips them back into position. Not a moment too soon, they catch the pedals and absorb his landing.

Holy hell. The guy's a machine.

He skids to a stop a bit farther down from Mitch, who breaks into a full grin.

"Nice," he says. He looks back up the hill. I follow his stare and see Rico hammering off the same jump that Chase just took. He shoots off the lip and gains air. But instead of clapping his feet together, Rico just lifts his feet off the pedals and out to the side, like a jumping jack. His feet come down just in time to catch his landing. It's a bit rough, but he sticks it.

Fantastic.

Seth, Nolan and I cheer. I want to try that.

I walk my bike up.

I go slower over the big jumps at first. I don't get as much air as Rico and Chase, and certainly not as much as Mitch, but my form is good. The more jumps I take, the faster I go, and the more comfortable I feel with it. After a while things seem to slow down a bit, and I can make decisions in midair. It feels like I've got time to try different things. I experiment, popping up and turning my handlebars a bit. Sweeping my tail out.

Rico keeps surprising all of us, pulling out crazy tricks and trying new stuff. He's fearless, but he's not stupid. He's completely focused on what he's doing. In the zone. He doesn't think about the other people who are standing around watching. He just drops in, does his shred and pulls off to hear what Mitch has to say. I admire him. Especially when he pops off a jump and twists his bike from side to side before landing it.

Seth is different. He's so used to being the center of attention that he can't focus on just doing his own thing. He hucks himself off jumps with a banshee screech, more intent on making it big than on getting it right. Ironically, he suffers the most run-ins with the forest floor because he's so keen on showing off. Whatever. He seems like he's having a good time.

I'm fully blown away when, just before lunch, Mitch takes me aside and tells me that I've got the makings of a competitive mountain biker. Maybe even a freerider.

"You think?" I ask.

Mitch nods. "Yeah. I've been watching everyone here. You seem to have an intuitive understanding of when to unleash it and when to rein it in, Jamie."

I feel my face growing warm, and I grin under his praise.

"Cool," I say. "What about Rico? He looks pretty great too." I glance over my shoulder to where Rico and Chase are replacing the tube in a blown tire.

"Rico too," agrees Mitch. "He's got guts. But your technique is smooth. Doesn't take you long to get a move dialed."

I feel suddenly tall. So tall. Like I could reach up and pick the sun out of the sky.

"Thanks, Mitch," I say.

He nods and claps me on the back. "Keep at it. You don't need to do anything fancy," he says. "Just keep doing what you're doing. You should check out some of the junior competitions."

"Yeah?" I ask. I'm about to ask him how he managed to get sponsors when Seth roars up and slides to a stop. Gravel pings off his spokes.

"Hey, Mitch," he pants. "Did you see me wave back there? I took my hands right off the bars."

"Did you, Seth?" Mitch asks. "That's great."

I leave Seth yapping at Mitch and head back into the jumps.

I drop off a lip and coast around, soaring over bumps, my head in the clouds. Mitch Woodgrove thinks I've got what it takes to ride competitively! I steal a glance over to where he's still having his ear bent by Seth. Maybe I can be like him one day and do this stuff for a living. Maybe I can get sponsorships to pay my race fees and help me get through university. Maybe I'll be rich!

chapter nine

We stay at the jump park for the whole day. We break for lunch, sitting in a loose group on a bunch of stumps and logs. When there's a break in the conversation, I decide to ask Mitch about his sponsorships. He must have some great backing, because all his gear is top-notch. And he drives a brand-new Toyota Tundra. And I heard him telling Chase earlier that he doesn't work at a day job.

Seth beats me to it. "So, Mitch," he says. "Is it hard to get good sponsorships?"

Mitch shakes his head. "Not really," he says. "Not if you're good." He glances at me.

I grin and open my mouth, but Nolan's jumping in now. "You must make a lot of money from your sponsors, then, eh?" he asks. "To pay for all that primo gear?"

I'm embarrassed for Mitch at this question. I guess Nolan doesn't think it's rude to ask pointed questions about how much people make. But, honestly, I'm wondering the same thing. Maybe sponsorship is the key to making millions.

Mitch isn't fazed by Nolan's nosiness. "Sponsorship is enough to keep you in good gear," he agrees. "And they pay for your races and travel. But that's about it. It can be hard to make a living just out of racing."

"But how can you survive, then?" Rico wants to know. "If you're always training, when do you work at a regular job? How do you pay your bills?"

Mitch shrugs. "I don't exactly live in a mansion. And I make a mean pot of KD!" Suddenly Seth sits forward. "Hey, you guys," he begins in an *I'm-going-to-tell-you-a-secret* tone. "You'll never believe what me and Jamie saw when we were out biking last night." I look sharply at Seth, but he's not looking in my direction.

"Seth," I say too loudly.

Everyone swivels their heads to look at me. Seth's eyes widen as he realizes his mistake. I can feel Mitch's eyes boring into me.

Nolan looks from Seth to me. "What?" he says. "What did you guys see?"

I think fast. "You know we weren't going to tell anyone about the bear scare, Seth," I say.

Seth's quick to catch on to my lie. "Oh," he says. "Sorry, man. I forgot." He fakes a worried glance at Chase and lets me steer the story. I breathe a sigh of relief.

"Duh," I say, pretending to be irritated with him.

Our ruse worked. I've moved the topic away from drugs and toward something different. Of course, in mentioning bears, I've now got Chase's attention. I'll have to think something up on the fly. Damn Seth, anyway.

"You guys saw a bear?" Chase demands. "Why didn't you tell us?"

"Because it was small," I say. "And it was far away. Just a yearling, I'd say."

"Yep," Seth says. "It ran away when it caught sight of us. We must've scared it off."

I can't resist his setup. "Scared *you* pretty good, little brother," I tease. "You should've seen your face." I turn to the others. "Seth was completely freaked. Nearly pissed his pants."

"Oh, whatever," Seth scoffs. "I did not."

"Yeah," says Rico. "I noticed you were acting a bit weird after you came back from your ride yesterday. Thought you might have seen something while you were off in the trees."

Mitch looks at us. "You guys should be careful about going into parts of the forest you're not familiar with," he says. His smile is gone, and his face is deadly serious. "You never know what you might run into."

Seth stares at Mitch. I nod, dry-mouthed, unable to find any words to reply.

"That's true," says Chase. "You should always make as much noise as you can while you're in the trees. If a bear knows you're coming, she'll get out of your way. They don't like running into us any more than we like running into them."

Mitch stretches like a lazy cat. "Well," he says. "You guys up for another afternoon of humping and bumping?"

"Hell yeah," says Rico.

"Bring it!" shouts Nolan.

Seth and I exchange a nervous glance before packing up the remains of our lunch and following the others back into the bike park. That was a little too close for comfort.

After lunch, we work hard on our bikes. Up, down, up, down. Nobody breaks anything, but there are a fair number of cuts and bruises. Mitch takes a few jumps where he turns his whole bike around in a 360 underneath him. Maybe even two. I can't tell because it goes so fast. He shows us a few flips too. They're crazy great, but I can't even imagine how he found the courage to ever try his first one. He watches all of us as we ride, giving us tips and telling us when things are really working.

I'm still nervous about what went on between us at lunch, but Mitch is acting like nothing happened. Gradually, I relax back into a fun day of biking.

Mitch talks a lot about safety, and how important it is to stay in control. "I know you guys hate to hear it," he says, when we've taken a break to patch our broken, oozing skin, "but you've got to stay in control. Go slow, especially if you're on a trail you don't know or if you're trying a trick for the first time. Don't be stupid like me," he says.

Nolan raises his eyebrows. "*Mitch Woodgrove* and *stupid* don't seem to go together in the same sentence," he says.

Mitch shrugs. "See these teeth?" he asks, giving us a wide grin.

We look. His teeth seem perfect. Straight, even and white.

"Not yours?" asks Rico.

Mitch shakes his head.

"What happened?" Nolan wants to know. He's fishing around in his bag of trail mix, chasing a blue M&M. He pops it into his mouth and squints through smudgy glasses at Mitch's teeth.

"Entered a dip too fast on a trail I didn't know," Mitch replies. "I bombed into it, hard. My front shocks squished out. No bounce left in them. I flew over the handlebars and took a digger, right into the other side." He smacks the top of his helmet to show us the way he hit the wall. "Hammered it, square on," he continues. He opens his mouth and points to his front teeth. "Cracked all four of my teeth on the top," he says.

I grimace. "Ouch."

Seth shudders. "Gross." His hand goes to his mouth.

"Yeah, gross *and* ouch," Mitch agrees. "Lucky I didn't have my tongue between my teeth right then. I'd have bitten it in two."

It's quiet for a moment as we consider this.

"Nice," says Nolan. "Thanks for the image, Mitch." He turns to the side and pretends to yark.

Mitch laughs. "Let me be a lesson to you guys. Stay in control. You might not look as cool as you would if you were hammering... but you never look cool as Captain Crash."

chapter ten

The day is over long before I want it to be.

Chase asks Mitch whether he'd like to stay for supper. Mitch shakes his head. "I've got to bounce," he says. "Got some stuff to do tomorrow." He looks around. "Nice spot up here though, isn't it?" he asks no one in particular. "You've got a great bunch of bikers here too, Chase," he continues, looking around at us. "There's some real talent here." He looks at me when he says this. I give a small nod in return.

Nolan doesn't look up from cleaning his glasses on his shirt. "Aw, shucks, Mitch, you're making me blush," he says. Everyone laughs.

Chase walks Mitch to the end of the valley we're camped in. I watch him leave, disappointed that the party's over.

We stretch our muscles out, trading stories of our experiences on the jumps. After a day like that, there's no way we'll be able to get out of our sleeping bags in the morning unless we've stretched.

Seth and I are on supper detail tonight. When we're all limbered up, we start our supper preparations. I rummage through our food bag in search of some ingredients to put our meal together. Looks like it's going to be spaghetti and tomato sauce. No meat. I sigh.

Chase rejoins us at the fire pit. "What's cooking, Jamie?"

"Spag," I say. "No meat though. Bummer."

"We've got that veggie meat," Chase reminds me. I brighten. Yeah, of course!

I had forgotten the little package of meatless ground beef we'd brought.

"That'll work," I say.

"We used to pack fresh meat on our hikes when I was at camp," Chase says. "We always had to cook it by the third day, because that's when it would start to go green."

"Ugh," says Seth, screwing up his face in disgust. "That's nasty, man."

Chase nods. "Yeah. The good old days," he says, "before we learned about food safety." He lies back on the gravel and props his head on his rolled-up fleece jacket. "I like watching you guys work. You're doing a good job."

"You're just lazy," I say.

Chase spreads his hands in mock help-lessness. "Hey, it's the counselor's job. How can I supervise you if I'm too busy helping?"

I laugh.

Nolan rolls his bike up to the fire pit. "I'm starving," he says, snagging a piece of carrot from the pile Seth is chopping. "Glad you guys're cooking tonight."

"Where are you headed?" Chase asks, looking up. A flame of worry blooms inside me at his words. I had forgotten all about freebies. Nolan and Rico get to go off exploring now. I'm worried that Nolan and Rico will go down that trail, even though Seth and I tried to make it sound lame and boring when we got back to camp last night.

Nolan's next words calm my worries. "Can we go back to the jumps?" he asks.

"Hmm," says Chase. "If you're doing tricks, you should probably have me with you. No offense, Rico, but you're still in training. And to tell you the truth, gentlemen," he says, lacing his fingers behind his head, "I'm pretty comfy." He closes his eyes. "I don't exactly feel like getting back on my bike."

"We won't get hurt," says Nolan. "Rico's a counselor. And I'm totally Mr. Cautious and In Control."

Seth laughs. "Mr. Falling On His Ass is more like it," he says. "Don't forget, Nolan, we've all seen your true colors."

Nolan raises his chin and peers down his nose at Seth. "It was a moment of weakness, I'll admit," he says. "Seriously though, Chase. We'll be careful. It's only three minutes away. If one of us gets hurt, the other can bike back for help."

Chase thinks about this for a moment. "You got your first-aid kit, Rico?" he asks.

Rico nods and pats the bag on his back.

"I want you catching lighter air than we did today," says Chase. "No funny stuff. And I want you back here at six."

Nolan digs for his watch under his glove strap. "Hey, that's only half an hour," he protests. "The other guys got way longer last night."

"Yeah, and look at what they ran into," says Chase. "A bear, out foraging at dusk. Not cool." He shakes his head. "You've got half an hour. Twenty-nine minutes, now that you've spent one of them arguing with me."

Nolan sighs and grabs his handlebars. "Half an hour," he agrees. I listen to the crunch of gravel under his wheels as he rolls away.

Half an hour comes and goes. Nolan and Rico have yet to return.

"They're probably so stoked on the jump park that they've lost track of time," says Seth. "That place is wicked awesome."

"It was wicked awesome to have Mitch come and hang out with us," I say. I'm about to ask Chase what he thinks of the stuff Mitch was talking about at lunch, but Seth goes off on me.

"Yeah, you're his little pet biker, aren't you?" Seth asks. "He thought you were just the shit, didn't he?" He's half joking, but it makes me mad all the same. I shouldn't let it get to me, but I can't help myself.

"You're just choked that you couldn't make him fall in love with you, like you can with everyone else," I say.

Seth narrows his eyes at me. I'm pretty much the only person who can push

Seth's buttons. I can see he's trying to decide whether to get into it or not. He glances at Chase, who's stretched out on the ground nearby. I think he's asleep. "Whatever, Jamie." He lets it go. I let it go. We work in silence for a while. Seth walks to our sump spot and pours the water off the noodles.

I glance at the sun. It's already edged down behind the mountains. "They're late," I say. "Doesn't seem like Rico to miss curfew. Nolan maybe, but not Rico."

Seth shrugs. He's still too mad to talk.

I let a few more minutes slide by. Then I remember the computer on Chase's bike. He was showing it off today at lunch. It logs miles, checks your heart rate, maps terrain and shows you where you're going. I'm sure it could tie your shoes too, if you let it. But I know for a fact it has a clock on it.

I go to where Chase's bike is resting against a tree near the tents. The screen is blank, but as soon as I touch it, the display lights up. 6:23. Holy smokes. Those guys have been gone for almost an hour.

I head back to the fire pit, a bad feeling

growing in my stomach. Suddenly I'm certain Nolan and Rico aren't at the jump park. "Seth, did you happen to notice which way Rico and Nolan went?"

He doesn't look up from where he's stirring spaghetti sauce on the stove. "They went to the jump park, didn't they?"

"That's where they *said* they were going," I say. I nudge Chase's foot gently with my toe. "Chase." I nudge harder. "Chase, wake up."

Chase opens his eyes and sits up. He shakes his head and passes a hand over his eyes. "What's up? What time is it?" He looks around. "Where are the others?"

"I don't know. I was just trying to figure that out. It's almost six thirty," I say.

"Six thirty?" Chase is on his feet. "Where the hell are those guys?" Without waiting for an answer, he jogs off to get his bike. "I'm going out to the jump park to see what's what." He shoulders his pack and mounts up. "You guys stay put."

"Sure thing," says Seth.

"Be right here," I add. And then he's gone.

chapter eleven

Five minutes later, Chase is back. "They're not there," he says. His voice is clipped, angry. "Where the hell are they?"

Seth and I exchange glances. Then Seth looks at the ground. My stomach drops. I don't even have to ask. Damn.

He spilled it to the others.

"The grow-op," I say. "I *knew* you couldn't keep it quiet, Seth." I'm fuming, but Chase is even angrier.

"What?" Chase barks. "What grow-op?" He looks from me to Seth, then back at me. "What *grow-op*, Jamie?" He's almost shouting.

We don't have much time to waste. If those guys have somehow found their way out to the grow-op, they might be in big trouble right now.

I take a deep breath and tell Chase everything that happened last night. The single track, the double track, the dozens and hundreds and thousands of plants. Our race home. I watch his face flip-flop between anger and worry.

"Why the hell didn't you tell me about this?" Chase asks when I've finished. "What were you thinking?"

"We weren't thinking," I admit.

"We were worried that you'd make us pack up and leave," says Seth. "And that if we left, we would miss our chance to go biking with Mitch Woodgrove."

Chase is quiet for a moment. He shakes his head and then squeezes his temples. He looks at me. "I'm disappointed in you,

Jamie," he says gravely, "I thought you had better judgment than this." My ears grow hot, and I drop my eyes.

"Seth," Chase barks.

"Yeah?"

"Throw me my pack. I'm calling the camp. We need to get those guys out of there. We need help."

Seth tosses Chase his pack. Chase unzips it and digs for the sat phone. A second later he hauls it out, presses the power button and starts dialing.

The display doesn't light up.

I watch as Chase presses the buttons harder. Nothing. "It's not working," he says. His voice is calm, but I know he's worried.

He turns the phone over and pushes the power button again.

Still nothing.

He presses it again, holding it longer this time. I bite back on my panic, reminding myself that some phones need to have the power button pressed for a few seconds before they'll fire up.

Still nothing.

"Is it on?" Seth asks. He comes closer. "It is working?"

"I don't think so," Chase says. "The batteries must be dead."

"Do you have spares?" I ask.

Chase shakes his head. "Nope. They're supposed to check everything out and make sure all our equipment is in working order before we go off on out-trips," he says. He blinks, obviously surprised that the camp sent him out with subpar equipment. Then he looks up. "What about you guys? You got spares?"

I shake my head. The only stuff we have with us that takes batteries are our head-lamps, and those take tiny triple-As. No use in a sat phone.

"I don't, either," says Chase. "Let's check Nolan's and Rico's bags."

Our search turns up nothing.

We're stranded in a high mountain pass with no phone, no batteries. No way to call for help. And our friends are god knows where, very possibly in deep trouble.

"I'm going to kill those guys," Chase says. "Especially Rico."

"If the grow-op guys don't kill them first," says Seth, putting words to the fear that's suddenly settled in each of our hearts.

"Shut up, Seth," I say.

"What?" he asks. "It's not like we're not all worried about it."

Chase is deep in thought as we argue, the heels of his hands pressed against his eyes. After a moment, he looks up. "I'm going after them."

Seth turns on him. "What? Are you *crazy*? No, let's...let's wait a little while. Maybe they're on their way back now!"

I shake my head. "I doubt it, Seth. I think something's happened."

Chase glances at the computer on his bike. "It's after seven. We'll be losing daylight soon. I think that spells trouble."

Seth shifts uneasily on his feet. "But you can't just leave us here!"

Chase runs his hands through his hair. "I have no other choice now," he says. "It's a tough call, but I can't take you with me.

It's too late to bike out and go for help. It'll be dark soon, and the risk of getting lost is just too great. And besides, anything could happen to those two in the time it takes us to bike all the way back to camp from here. It would take us hours. Even longer in the dark." Chase breaks off and looks toward the trees. "You two will be fine to look after yourselves until I get back. I know you will. You're both sensible guys with good outdoor skills. If we're lucky, those two have just had an accident. Broken an ankle or something. But if something is wrong—you know, *really* wrong—I don't need to be dragging you guys into it."

"He's right, Seth," I say. "It's too dangerous for us all to go."

"Besides," Chase continues, "what if they do come back? Someone needs to be here, or else they'll go looking for us. And then we'll *all* be separated. And that's dangerous." He pulls his helmet on and buckles it.

I nod. What he's saying makes sense. I don't like the idea of splitting up, but it's the only choice we have right now.

"Where am I going?" Chase asks me.

"Head straight on the single track for about two miles, then take the fork toward the forest on the left," I say. "The trail opens up into a double track pretty quick. The plants start growing right there. We went a few hundred feet before we turned around and came back."

"Okay," Chase says, sliding his shoe onto his pedal. He looks at us. At Seth's worried face. "Don't worry," he says. "I'm coming right back. And I'll be dragging their sorry asses with me."

I nod again, my stomach knotting into a tight ball. It feels terrible to have our counselor go off into the forest in the fading daylight. To go and find who knows what.

What if he doesn't come back?

I push the thought away. Of course he'll come back. He's Chase, man. He's a machine. Super Chase.

Seth and I watch him pedal toward the path that leads straight into the heart of danger.

chapter twelve

Seth and I have a whole feast laid out for us, but neither of us can do more than pick at our spaghetti. I finally scoop everything into one pot and put a lid on it. We'll keep it in case everyone comes back ravenous. Or else we'll put it in a ziplock bag and stick it in the bear hang.

I really hope that's not what happens.

We wash our plates and the pots without talking. I take out a deck of cards.

"Want me to boil some water for hot chocolate?" Seth asks.

I shake my head. It wouldn't feel right to be sitting here, safe and warm and drinking hot chocolate when the other guys are who knows where. Probably not drinking hot chocolate. Besides, I don't feel like anything sweet right now.

We play Crazy Eights and Twenty-One, the only games we know.

Gradually, the sky darkens.

Seth watches, chin on his arms, as I build a fire. As the flames lick up through the tinder and ignite the larger pieces of wood, I look up and see the first star shining in the faded purple sky. Jesus. Where *are* those guys?

"Where *are* those guys?" Seth asks. I'd smile if I weren't so worried right now. We might not always get along, but we sure think the same way sometimes.

"I don't know," I say. I sit beside him and watch the flames as they reach higher.

"How long do you think Chase has been gone?"

I look around at the sky. "I'd say it's close to eight thirty now."

Seth shivers. "Why isn't he back, Jamie?"

I take a deep breath and shake my head. "I don't know." I've never hated hearing those words so much.

"Do you think something's happened?"

I don't want to admit it, but I'm terrified that something has. And I don't know what to do next. Do we stay here and wait longer? Try to go after Chase? Send up smoke signals?

Seth stands suddenly, snatching up the sat phone from where it's sitting on a nearby stump. "Stupid phone," he hisses. "Stupid idiots back at camp. How stupid do you have to be to send a bunch of kids into the wilderness with emergency equipment that doesn't even work?" Seth asks. "Now what are we going to do?" His voice is rising, panicky.

He turns toward the mountains at the end of the valley. "This sucks!" he screams. His words travel back to him in a faint echo. The cords stand out on his neck as he screams it again, louder. "This SUCKS!"

He turns and throws the phone to the ground. The back of the battery compartment pops off, and the batteries spill out onto the hard earth.

I jump up and grab the phone. "Don't do that, Seth," I say. I put the batteries into my jacket pocket. "You don't know if we'll need that thing later."

"Oh, and it'll be so useful without any batteries, won't it?" Seth spits. He sits down and puts his head on his arms.

"Listen, man, it's not my fault there's no juice."

Seth lifts his head. "Well, can't you fix it?" he barks. "Jamie the Perfect? You're so good at everything else. Can't you just snap your fingers and make new batteries appear, Jamie? Can't you summon us a new phone with the staggering powers of your mind?"

I stare at him. "What are you talking about?"

"You're always the one with A Solution To The Problem," Seth says, putting air quotes around the words. "Everyone looks up to you because you're so smart," he says.

"Even Mom and Dad." He looks away and rubs his eyes with the fingers of one hand. A frustrated sob escapes him. I'm speechless. I know he's worried about our situation, and I am too, but...*this* is what eats Seth up inside? That I'm smart? I mean, I've always gotten top marks in school. But I don't brag about it. I offer to help him with his schoolwork, and he used to let me, but he doesn't want me to anymore. Now Seth just struggles along on his own, barely scraping out a passing grade. It would be so much easier if he would let me go over the things he doesn't get the first time around in class. But he doesn't ever let me.

"Who cares if I'm smart, Seth?" I say. "Everybody loves *you*. You're, like, Mr. Popularity. I don't have a quarter of the friends you have."

"Yeah, well. Friends can't help you get into the Faculty of Engineering," he says. He won't look at me. "You need good marks for that."

Engineering. I had no idea he still wanted to do that. When Seth was little, all he did was build intricate things. He built the craziest stuff out of Lego. It was amazing. We all used to say he'd be an architect when he grew up.

But when he started middle school, Seth stopped talking about being an engineer. He struggled to keep up his marks in math and science. And then, a couple of years ago, he gave up on school altogether, turning his energies toward making friends and having fun.

I had no idea he still carried around that old dream.

Here I've been resenting Seth all this time for being popular, and he's been jealous of me for being smart! I feel like an idiot. But I can't think of what to say. For once, my "great mind" fails me.

And I'm still worried as hell about what's happening here.

This is all getting to be a bit much.

chapter thirteen

I sit back down by the fire and put my head in my hands. "I can't believe the camp would send us out with a dead phone."

"Yeah, well, they did," Seth says, his voice angry. "And no spare batteries. So where does that leave us?" He's almost shouting now. "We're in a real tidy heap of crap now, huh, Jamie? Our friends are lost in the forest at nighttime, in the middle of a massive grow-op with who knows how many armed guards." His voice rises, closing in on hysteria. "Maybe they're already all dead and lying there in pools of their own blood," he says, gesturing toward the ground, as though their bodies were right in front of us.

I wince at the thought. "Seth," I say.

He ignores me. "Maybe those guys are coming for *us* now," he says.

His last words fill me with cold dread. I sure hope not.

And then it dawns on me that no one else is coming to help us. Whatever happens next is our decision. The way this situation will shake out is entirely up to us. I take my head out of my hands and look at Seth.

"Seth," I say, keeping my voice calm. "Listen to me." I touch his arm. The words and my hand work like a magic salve, soothing him. He looks into my eyes. Listening. He doesn't listen much anymore, but he sure is now.

"We need to figure out what we're going to do," I say. "We need to make a plan. We can't just sit here."

He nods.

"Well, we *could* just sit here," I continue, "but I'm not sure that's our best option. The way I see it, we have three choices. One is to try to ride out to a road and then try to get help. But I have no idea where we are or how far in we've come. I wasn't paying attention when we drove up here. And then we biked for a full day to get in here. We could spend days on the logging roads and not see anyone."

"Oh, man," Seth groans.

I keep going. "Option two, we wait here until someone from camp comes looking for us. But we're on the second night of a four-day trip, so that means no one will even know we're missing until suppertime the day after tomorrow. That's over forty-eight hours until someone even launches a search. That feels like a long time to wait."

"What's option three?" Seth asks.

I take a steadying breath. "Option three is we go after them."

Seth swallows. Nods. Stares at the ground for a while. "It's what we've got to do, isn't it, Jamie?" He raises his eyes to meet mine.

I nod.

"Now?"

I look up at the sky. More stars have edged their way out of the blue velvet. The last of the daylight is a whitish fringe around the mountaintops. There's no moon tonight. It's bloody dark out here.

And it'll only be darker in the forest. Taking headlamps would be an exercise in stupidity. They'd turn us into easy targets in terrain that's completely unfamiliar to us. We would be at a distinct disadvantage.

I refuse to think about what—or who— would have the advantage.

I look back at Seth.

"We'll go at first light."

I'm sure I won't sleep well. But I am surprised when I wake early the next morning after a deep and dreamless sleep. I sit up and shake Seth, who's snoring beside me.

My body is sore from all of yesterday's action. I guess that's what made me sleep so soundly.

I give Seth another shake. "Seth," I say. "We've got to get going." My stomach does a slow rollover as I think about what I've left unsaid. *Hey, come on, little brother. Let's go ride to what could possibly be our deaths.*

I shouldn't think of it that way. There's any number of possible explanations for where Chase, Rico and Nolan might have gone. For all we know, they might have gotten lost and be waiting for us to come and find them. Not likely, considering Chase has GPS on his bike computer. Or maybe they all fell off a ledge and are hanging out with sprained and broken ankles, waiting for us to come and help them back to the campsite. Again, not likely that they'd all be injured at the same time. But still.

Or maybe they're dead.

I shove the thought away. I give Seth another shove too. "Get up, man. Come on. We've got to go find the others."

I stick my head out of the tent, half hoping that everyone has come home sometime in the night. My breath blows white in the frosty mountain air. I pull my tuque down tighter over my ears and unzip the rest of the door. Everything is exactly as we left it last night. Right down to the pot of spaghetti I forgot to put in the bear hang.

I kind of wish the bears had found it. Then maybe they could've finished us off too so we wouldn't have to face the task ahead.

Seth groans behind me. His sleeping bag rustles as he stretches. I rifle through my pack, mentally compiling a list of things we're going to need for today's mission.

I leave the tent and find a thirsty-looking tree to water. I zip up, then start filling my bag with emergency supplies. Headlamps. Duct tape. A large knife. Water bottles. Extra food. Rope. Emergency blankets. Jackets. The first-aid kit Mom made us pack.

Seth gets dressed while I use a pencil stub to scratch out a note on a pad of paper I found in the bottom of the first-aid kit.

August 9.

I glance at the sun's position in the sky.

6:45 AM. *My brother Seth and I have left this campsite to try and find our friend, Nolan, and our counselors, Rico and Chase.*

I am irritated with myself that I never asked for anyone's last name.

We are on a mountain-biking out-trip with Camp Edgelow. We've taken our bikes and followed the path that leads away from this campsite to the southeast. Two days ago, we discovered a large marijuana grow operation about two miles down this path, where it forks off from a dirt single track to an overgrown dual-track. The grow-op is most likely guarded, possibly by armed men. We think our friends have run into danger there. Our satellite phone died, and we don't know where we are. We don't feel it's safe to try to bike out of the mountains alone. We have gone to find our friends.

My hand shakes as I write the final few words.

Please send help. Jamie Gardiner.

I hear a noise behind me and turn. Seth's eyes shift from the paper to me.

"It's good," he says. "Let's hope someone finds it." He puts his hand on my shoulder.

I nod my head and fight the lump that has risen in my throat. What are we getting ourselves into?

I slide the note into a ziplock bag so that it won't get wet if it rains. I rip several pieces of duct tape off the roll and secure the note to the outside wall of our tent. We slip on our packs, buckle our helmets and wrestle our hands into gloves that are stiff from yesterday's sweat.

Without a word, we swing our legs over our bikes and pedal away from safety.

chapter fourteen

We cut through the still morning air. My fingers are stiff on the handlebars, partly because of the cold and partly from yesterday's play at the jump park. I think about that—how those might have been the last jumps Rico and Nolan will ever take.

And Chase.

My stomach is a bundle of live wires as we pedal silently along the hard dirt path. I slow as we approach where the double track crosses the trail. I squeeze my brakes and glide to a stop. Seth rolls up next to me, and we look around.

Right in front of us is the grow-op, neatly edged by the track. We never noticed it the other day until we were well into it because the cannabis is so well disguised by the trees. This is the far western edge of the grow. The double track must act like a perimeter route, containing the plants and providing an easy way for the growers to get around.

The thought of the growers sends electricity sparking through me. Who owns all this weed? Where are they going to sell it? Seth and I silently take in the scene in front of us. While some of the plants come up to our shoulders, a number of them reach much higher, over our heads. I wonder what the street value would be for a single stalk. Multiply that by a few hundred thousand and you're looking at a heavy suitcase full of cash.

Definitely an investment worth protecting.

"Let's stick together," I say. Seth nods.

I hold out my gloved fist. Seth bumps it with his.

"Showtime," I say.

We pedal slowly along the wide track that runs parallel to the marijuana. I strain my ears to listen for any sort of noise. We bike for a while, searching for something we don't yet know exists.

As the track curves around to the right, I realize I can't hear Seth behind me anymore. I glance back. He's not there. My heart skips a beat, then pounds out a couple of extras to make up for it.

Where the hell is Seth?

I haul on my brakes and turn my bike around.

Now I hear a noise. It's an engine. It sounds like it's far away. In the direction we just came from. My stomach drops uneasily. I can feel my palms breaking out in sweat. I wheel my bike back a bit on the path and peer around the curve.

Seth is a long way behind. He's picking something up off the ground. His water bottle. *God, just leave it, Seth!* The engine sounds like it's getting closer. Doesn't he hear it? I want to shout at him, tell him to get on his bike and get out of there—dive into the trees or something—but I'm afraid to draw attention to myself.

Seth hears the engine. I watch as he quickly replaces the water bottle and swings his leg over the crossbar. He punches on his pedals, holding his handlebars in a death grip. They jerk from side to side as his feet pound him out of there. But he's not thinking clearly. He can't outrun a motorized vehicle. And there's nowhere for him to hide on the track. He'd be better off ditching his bike and running into the forest, where he can climb a tree or tunnel into the undergrowth.

He's still pretty far away, but maybe I can communicate this to him. I wave my arm at him, pointing to the trees on the other side of the track. He sees me. He glances at the forest as I point to it, but he doesn't get the message. He keeps pedaling. I point him toward the forest again.

His head lifts, and I think he gets what I'm saying. Suddenly, the source of the engine noise reveals itself. My heart leaps into my throat. Right behind Seth, an ATV lurches out of a hidden pathway. A tall skinny guy with a camo jacket is driving. He catches sight of Seth and revs the engine. I see a flash of white teeth under the shadow of his cap.

My lungs refuse to collect any air. Hidden out of sight just beyond the curve, I watch the ATV roar up behind my brother. Seth's eyes turn to saucers. He pedals faster still. He keeps spinning as the ATV draws up beside him. When they're flush with each other, Seth looks over. The guy sneers at him. His mouth opens in a lopsided laugh as he edges the ATV closer to Seth. So close that it's almost touching his wheels. I watch, my heart in my throat, wondering how hard Seth will go down if this guy rubs him. Bones could break. Seth could even get run over.

But then Seth pulls a beautiful move, slamming on his brakes and throwing his bike to the ground in one quick movement. Before Skinny Guy knows what's happening, Seth is off, pelting for the trees.

Wicked.

But Skinny Guy is fast too. He grinds the machine to a stop. With a loud curse, he launches himself after Seth.

The ATV is left idling a mere stone's throw away from where I'm standing astride my bike. For a few spinning, breathless moments, I try to figure out what I should do. Should I take the vehicle?

But that's a dumb idea. Where would I take it? And besides, I'm not leaving unless Seth is with me. Should I run into the forest and help Seth? But then if Seth and I both get caught, there won't be anyone else to help find the others.

My brother is in danger.

So are three other people.

When I hear Seth's shout from just inside the trees, I make up my mind. Whether he drives me nuts or not, that's my baby brother. I'm going in to help him.

I drop my bike. I haven't even taken three steps when Seth emerges from the trees, arms pinned behind his back. He's being steered roughly by Skinny Guy, who's got one hand on Seth's head and one clamped around his wrists. It reminds me of those cop shows on TV where they always put their hands on the suspects' heads to push them into the squad car.

Skinny Guy's looking in the direction of the ATV. I hope he doesn't look my way.

"Little snoop," he growls. "That's four of you now. Buncha stupid kids. Who else are we going to find? Huh? Who else is out here?" he demands, giving Seth a shake. I wonder if the guy is armed. I can't see any gun, but that doesn't mean he doesn't have one.

Seth doesn't respond. Without moving his head, he turns his huge, frightened eyes toward me. I start to move toward him, but he gives his head the tiniest of shakes: no.

I stay where I am, concealed by the trees and the tall strong-smelling plants. I'll follow along behind them. That way I'll be able to figure out where everyone is. And then maybe I can try to do something about it.

Although what that would be, I don't know. I'm feeling pretty powerless right now.

Skinny Guy is ripping duct tape off a huge roll. He wraps Seth's wrists with it, muttering angrily as he works. He's rough. He indicates for Seth to sit on the metal rack in front of the ATV's handlebars. I watch as Skinny Guy jerks tape around Seth's ankles. Tight. I pray that Seth will be able to keep his balance on the front of the ATV. I see him reach down and grab hold of the rack to steady himself.

Skinny Guy guns the engine. A black cloud belches out of the tailpipe.

Fear squeezes my head as the seriousness of the situation hits me. Our friends are missing, most likely caught by this scary-looking guy. Or someone who works with him. My brother is hog-tied, perched on the front of an ATV. About to be transported who-knows-where by a thug whose job it is to guard a massive drug operation.

Things are looking pretty ugly right about now.

And if we're going to get out of this mess, it's up to me from here on in.

chapter fifteen

Without warning, I am seized by the shakes. Like there's a jackhammer inside my spinal cord. I fight for control. If I let them settle in, I'll be too freaked out to do anything useful.

Deep breath in. Deep breath out.

Come on, Jamie. Don't sketch now. People are relying on you.

Somehow the thought brings me back down. The tremors subside, and I force myself onto my bike.

I pedal along a fair distance back from the ATV. I keep an eye on Seth as the ATV bumps along. He seems to be managing okay. I can't believe what a crazy situation we've found ourselves in. I try not to think about our parents and what they would say if they had any idea what's going on.

I try, too, not to think about what I might find when we get to wherever we're going. I try not to imagine what possible help I'll be able to offer. I simply focus on pushing my feet around and around. Following the ATV so I can see where it's taking Seth.

At last we turn off the double track onto an old logging road. I stay well back. I pray there aren't other guards hanging out in the thickets of the grow-op.

The ATV stops in front of a small wooden cabin at the road's edge. It's about the size of a single garage. I wrestle my bike into the trees and watch. Skinny Guy is saying something to Seth, and Seth is shaking his head. Skinny Guy lets Seth jump down from the ATV. Seth stands up as well as he can with his ankles tied, and Skinny Guy slaps a piece of duct tape over his mouth. From his pocket he produces a folding knife. *A knife? Oh god.* My horror turns to relief as he reaches down and slices through the duct tape binding Seth's ankles. Then he gives Seth a sharp push toward the cabin. Seth knows enough not to look for me. I hope he knows I'm here. I can only imagine how terrified he's feeling right now.

I edge closer to the cabin. When the door closes behind Seth and his captor, I run forward quickly and quietly. I size up the cabin. There aren't any windows on this side. No one can look out and spot me dashing from tree to tree.

Three bikes are leaning up against the side of the building. Chase. Nolan. Rico. A mixture of relief and dread washes over me. Are they still alive?

My panic rises. What am I supposed to do now? Storm into the cabin and just... free everybody? From right under this ugly thug's nose?

No, wait. Make that *two* ugly thugs.

As I'm hiding and freaking out behind the trunk of a big fir, the door to the cabin opens and a second guy steps out onto the porch. He's wearing a black T-shirt and jeans. Biker boots. The bottom of his nose is pierced with a metal bar that curves downward, like an angry frown. He stretches as though he's just woken up from a long sleep. Even from my limited vantage point, I can see he's a big dude. A scary dude.

With one tattooed, well-muscled arm, he lifts a smoke to his mouth. Crams his hand into the pocket of his jeans and produces a lighter. He sparks up the cigarette and takes a deep pull. Skinny Guy comes back outside, closing the door behind him. Big Dude offers him the cigarette. Skinny Guy takes a puff and coughs a bit. Passes it back to Big Dude.

The smoke drifts toward me. It's sweet and peppery. I realize they're smoking a joint, not a cigarette. I don't smoke up, but I've been around people who do. My panic eases a little bit. This is good. They might be easier to *deal* with if they're stoned and slow moving.

Deal with them? How, exactly, am I supposed to *deal* with them?

As I'm wondering this, Big Dude hands Skinny Guy the joint and pulls a phone out of his back pocket. He pulls up the antenna and places a call. Waits for the satellites to align their signals. Skinny Guy smokes and looks around at the forest. When his head swivels in my direction, my heart leaps into my mouth. I jerk my head behind the tree and hold my breath.

I'm starting to feel a bit like James Bond.

As soon as the thought bubbles up, I grab on to it. I can do this. I'm just going to imagine that I'm some special-forces guy who does this kind of stuff for a living. Spies on people. Immobilizes thugs. Rescues his friends.

The thought calms me. My heart slows to a regular rhythm. My field of vision opens. I see more. My ears sharpen.

Something inside me hardens, steeling itself for what lies ahead.

Big Dude talks into the phone, his voice low and quiet. It bugs me that I can't hear the conversation. I decide to dash from the tree to where there's an opening under the porch of the cabin. It's a crazy place to go, since it's right under where they're standing, but there's nowhere closer where I can still remain hidden. I wait until Skinny Guy is looking the other way, and then I make a run for it. Silent as a ninja. Deadly as Bond.

I remove my pack and wiggle into the space under the stairs. The bikes lean against the cabin behind me. I could reach out and grab Nolan's water bottle if I wanted to.

In my new spot, I can look up through the floorboards of the porch. I don't let myself think about all the mutant insect life that might be down here with me.

Or dead bodies.

I shove the thought down, straining to catch bits of the conversation overhead.

"Yeah, the first two showed up last night. That's when we grabbed them...Yeah, but then another one showed up, like, an hour later...Yeah, of course...No, but then this morning the other kid showed up. Damian got him and brought him back here...Yeah, some kind of camp is what one of them told me...No, there aren't any more." He raises his eyebrows at Skinny Guy—Damian—who blows out a thin stream of smoke and shakes his head. "Yeah, I'm sure, Deuce," says Big Dude.

Butterflies take flight in my stomach. Whoever this Deuce guy is, he suspects there are still other kids on the loose. He's going to tell these guys to be on high alert, watching. I have to be supercareful.

"Okay, we'll keep an eye out for any others...Yeah, we'll hold those four for ya," says Big Dude. He gives the thumbs-up to Damian, who looks relieved. "Sounds good. Yeah, okay. No, they're all tied up inside. They're not talking. They can't.

We taped them." Damian smirks and takes a drag.

Still listening, Big Dude glances at his watch. "You coming out? Okay...Wow, that's really soon. No, no, it's cool, I'm just saying...Okay, sure thing, Deuce. See you later."

Big Dude folds the phone up and places it on the porch railing. He reaches for the joint. "He's on his way."

"He's early," says Damian, passing it over. "He wasn't supposed to come until tomorrow."

Big Dude shrugs. "Whatever, man. Deuce is in charge of his own schedule. He sounded a bit pissed with this whole thing about the kids."

"Well, it's hardly our fault that we found those stupid punks snooping," whines Damian.

"Deuce doesn't care whose fault it is," says Big Dude. "If he's mad, it's best just to stay the hell out of his way." He pauses for a drag. "I'm glad he's coming. Let him deal with the nosy kids."

Damian nods. "Yeah. Otherwise we'd have to do it all. And I don't want the blood of four people on my hands."

I shudder. So the only reason these guys haven't killed the others yet is because they're waiting for their boss to come and do it? I close my eyes and fight the swimmy feeling inside my head.

Damian continues, "Yeah, no thanks. I think I'd rather sleep at night. Got to make it to heaven." He yawns and rubs his face.

Big Dude laughs and claps Damian on the shoulder. "You're in the wrong line of work, then, sissy boy."

Damian gives him a little shove. "Speak for yourself, Warren. It's not like you want to kill a bunch of kids either."

Warren shrugs and passes the joint to Damian, who shakes his head. Warren shrugs again, takes the last pull and stubs it out on the railing. He tosses it into the grass in front of the cabin. "I do what I have to do," he says, exhaling a stream of smoke.

"When did Deuce say he's going to be here?" Damian asks.

"Ten," Warren replies.

Ten! I look up at the sky, but I can't see the position of the sun. I think back to what's happened so far this morning since Seth and I left the campsite. I figure we left just before seven. I can't imagine that more than an hour has passed, so that puts us at almost eight.

I have two hours to get everyone out of here before this Deuce guy shows up and picks everybody off.

"I'm gonna go find out from one of these kids how many others are still out there," says Warren. "Because I get the feeling we're not done yet. And we'd damn well better figure it out before Deuce gets here." He turns and goes back inside, slamming the cabin door behind him.

chapter sixteen

Damian yawns again and then comes down the stairs off the porch. He strolls over to a tree and unzips his pants. This is my chance, I realize. I've got to put him out of commission so that I've only got Warren left to deal with.

Adrenaline surges through my body. I look wildly around. There's nothing under the stairs I can use as a weapon. No stick. No large rocks. Nothing on the ground beside me either. I start to panic, but then

I think of James Bond. The fuzz in my brain clears. I realize the perfect weapon is right in front of my eyes.

Without a second's hesitation, I grab the seat of Nolan's bike. My other hand works furiously to unscrew the saddle from the seat post. Lucky for Damian, Nolan's got a skinny ass, so he's got a padded seat. Still heavy, though, even with all that gel inside.

I slide the seat out of the post just as Damian gives himself a shake. As he's zipping up, I slip up behind him. My foot hits a twig and snaps it. Suddenly alert, he turns, reaching around his back for something.

His gun.

Soundlessly, before he can get his hand into his belt, I bring the seat down, smashing it across the side of his head.

He goes down like a moose that's been shot. I blink, amazed I did that so easily. A trickle of spit eases out of Damian's mouth. I wonder if I killed him. I hope not. I only wanted to knock him out. I'm not that experienced with hammering people upside the head with bike seats, so there's a possibility that I might have gone overboard.

I need something to tie him up with. I turn and run back to my pack. I rip open the top. My hands close around the coil of rope. I grab the roll of duct tape too. Moving quickly, I return to where Damian is now moaning faintly. Good. I didn't kill him.

I pray that the door to the cabin doesn't open.

I take both of Damian's hands. He's heavy for a skinny guy. I drag him over to his own dark pee spot, leaning him against the tree trunk. Suddenly I remember his gun. I pull up the back of his shirt and feel gingerly around. Don't want to shoot off a finger. There it is, tucked into his belt. I shiver to think how close I came to getting shot.

I yank the gun out of his belt and put it on the ground. I stare at it. That's the first time I've ever touched a gun. It's fully weird, but I can't stop to think about it right now.

I pull Damian's hands around the back of the tree and wrap them tightly with the rope. I tie a firm knot and tuck the loose ends where his fingers can't reach them. As I work, I glance back at the cabin. If Warren comes out, I want to see him.

When Damian is tied, I grab the duct tape and tear off a strip. The noise is loud in the quiet morning air, and it shocks me. I freeze and stare at the cabin door. Another bolt of adrenaline enters my system, and my heart starts to skip all over the place. The door doesn't open.

Keep your cool, Jamie.

I stick the duct tape over Warren's mouth, pressing down hard. He moans, but he's still out. His head lolls to the side. I can see a nasty bump rising where I hit him. He'll have a bad headache later. Even worse once Deuce is through with him.

Thinking about Deuce makes me move faster. I check Damian's body to see whether he has any other weapons on him. I don't find any, but I do find the keys to the ATV. I put them in my pocket.

I take the gun and leave him there, tied to the tree in the early August sunshine. I don't know what to do with the gun, so I put it under the porch. As an after-thought, I grab the sat phone from the deck railing and stuff it into my pocket along with the keys.

I'm not sure what to do next, so I stand beside the cabin wall and try to think. I don't want to go into the cabin yet, not with Warren there. I want to call for help on the phone, but I'm worried that he'll hear me.

I'm having trouble figuring this all out. What would 007 do?

As my exhausted mind slogs its way through the options, I realize I'm terribly thirsty. I haven't had much water since yesterday. And I was sweating buckets at the bike park. I lean over and yank the water bottle off Rico's bike. It's half full. I unscrew the lid and drink until the bottle is nearly empty. As I screw the lid back on, the metal bottle slips from my grasp and clangs to the rocky ground below me.

Shit.

chapter seventeen

I freeze, plastered against the cabin wall, my mouth an O of fear. A second passes. I am unable to breathe.

When the door yanks open behind me, I realize I've got to get my ass out of here before I get killed. I make a split-second decision. I grab the closest bike.

Crap! There's no seat!

I fling it away and reach for the next one. I hope its parts are all working.

I take two quick steps, swing myself on and pedal like hell. I see now I'm on Chase's bike. Behind me, I hear Warren shouting, but I'm working too hard to hear what he's saying. I touch the computer screen, and the map function pops up.

A sudden gunshot splits the air. Okay, forget the computer. My heart pummels against the walls of my chest. *He's shooting at me!* As the words roll out of my brain, I feel something hit the back of my bike. A bullet! I downshift, put my head down and pedal faster than I ever have before.

It hits me that I should try to be a moving target. I zig and zag so Warren can't train his gun on me.

The bike's been hit, but I can't tell where. Not my tire, because I'm still rolling. Not my gears, because I just shifted cleanly. And Warren didn't shoot *me*, because all my parts are still working and nothing hurts. Maybe it was a rock being kicked up from the ground or something. It's not like I'm about to stop and look.

I listen with dread for the sound of the ATV behind me, but it doesn't come. Oh, yeah—I've got the keys in my pocket. This makes me smile. Score one for Jamie.

What I *do* hear behind me is Warren swearing. I risk a quick backward glance. He's jumped onto one of the other bikes and is pounding after me.

I'm fast, but Warren is strong. And I don't want to run the risk that he'll overtake me on this path. Besides, he's got a gun. The closer I let him get to me, the greater the chances are that he'll try to shoot me again.

I definitely don't feel like getting shot today.

Something in this scene's going to have to change. I keep an eye out as I pelt along, looking for side trails. The double track runs along the top of a pretty good hill. If I can find a way to start us dropping through the trees, I should be able to outmaneuver this guy. Assuming he isn't a pro downhiller. Which he could well be, given his ripped physique.

But something tells me he's more of a barbell bozo than a biker.

Just as the panic is about to creep back in, I fly past a side trail. It's a small track, more like an overgrown deer path, but it leads in the right direction. I squeeze my brakes hard. And suddenly I understand what the bullet hit.

My rear brakes are gone. There's no speed-check action back there, whatsoever. The only brakes I have left are on the front. And those aren't what I'm going to need when I'm leading an armed criminal on a steep downhill chase through unfamiliar terrain.

All these thoughts race through my head as I turn my bike around and point it down the deer path. I don't take another second to consider my options—like there are any in the first place—because Warren is bearing down on me, hard. I glance down the trail, then back at Warren. He raises his arm and points his gun.

I drop down the hillside, aware that this might be the last ride of my life.

chapter eighteen

Things start to happen really fast. The long grass lies flat across the trail, concealing the rocks and roots below. I remind myself to stay loose, letting my body absorb whatever bumps I hit.

I'm tempted to just blaze and get the hell out of this guy's sight. But Nolan's spectacular face-plant flashes in my mind's eye. I don't want to take any soil samples today, thanks. There won't be anybody at the bottom to patch me up. I have to remember what Mitch said, and stay in control.

But I also have to stay alive.

And there's a dude with a gun behind me. And he's pretty steamed.

I listen for Warren, but it's hard to hear anything above the sound of my own descent. I doubt he's coordinated enough to shoot me while navigating a narrow section of downhill. The path is working in my favor.

My front wheel hits a hidden rock and I wobble. Death cookie. A bolt of fear shoots through me. I refocus my attention on the path ahead. I hope Warren hits the same rock and pitches over his handlebars.

Another trail joins the path and it widens. I ride gratefully into a section of hard packed dirt. This seems like a proper bike trail. I send out a message of thanks for all the great single track out here on the North Shore.

I'm not sure where this path is taking me, but that doesn't matter right now. As long as it keeps going. I look ahead.

The trail seems pretty clear, so I punch it. I'm taking it pretty gonzo right now, but I can't afford to slow down. I push all thoughts of falling out of my mind and focus on being one with the trail. I roll along, up rises and into dips like a wave following the ocean floor. I steal a peek behind me, the wind rushing through my helmet openings.

Warren has dropped back. He's slowed down to take the hill. Good. I've bought myself some time. I'm formulating a devious plan. If it works the way I want it to, I'll be able to put Warren away too. Without getting myself killed in the process.

As if the universe has heard my thoughts, a perfect drop appears ahead of me. From where I am, it looks like it's about three feet high—high enough to really mess someone up if they don't know what they're doing. Only problem is, it could mess me up too. Not because of the drop—I can handle that—but because it's a supershort landing. About twenty feet below the ledge, the path whips away to the left.

Along the edge of a cliff.

If I don't make the turn, I'll pitch straight over the cliff and into the trees. I have no idea what's below, but from past experience, I can pretty much guess that it's rocks, trees...and more rocks and trees. Not a very soft landing.

I shift my weight onto my rear tire and squeeze my front brake a bit to slow me down. It's all I've got—and it's the lesser of two risks. I can't afford to take this drop at full speed. If I did, I'd drill straight into the forest and end up bringing home a Christmas tree, like Seth did last year. He flailed into the bushes and came out with little branches stuck in his helmet and gloves and shirt. I had a good time teasing him about it.

Except Seth didn't break any arms or legs when he did his bit of pruning.

If I crater, the story will have a different ending.

There's another reason I can't afford to bag out on the landing. If I do, my plan will fail.

And there are four other people whose lives are depending on me right now.

As I near the drop, I imagine Mitch coaching me through it. I loosen up on the approach, wiggling my butt back on the seat and stretching out my arms ahead of me. Loose elbows. All the outside noise falls away. I look at the path ahead, picking my line and scouting the exact spot where I'm going to set down.

Then I hit the jump, and boost.

Airborne.

I watch the corner drawing closer. I'm wishing I'd come into it slower before launching off that big-ass lip. As I coast through the air, I see that the gravel below me is thick and slippery.

I'm going to slide.

I force my muscles to relax again. I need to flow with the skid when I come down.

My front and rear wheels make contact with the ground at the same time. Nice. And not a second too soon. I need to turn. Like, right now.

Gravel spurts away from my wheels with a loud *shhhisshh*. As I hit, I lean slightly to the left. This sends the tail of my bike to the right. My back wheel fishtails. I instinctively put my left foot on the ground to offer a third point of contact to stabilize the bike in its slide. So far, so good. I crank my handlebars to the left. My front tire obeys, but not before it slips on the rolling gravel.

With both wheels unstable, I grind my foot into the ground and prepare for the fall. I let go of the handlebars and allow the bike to slide away from under me. My other foot and my hands all hit the ground at the same time. The gravel absorbs my wipeout. I absorb some gravel in my knees. I flail for a second, looking for my balance.

Then I'm up, adrenalized, turning to see where my bike landed. It's near the edge of the drop-off. I grab it and check it over.

Not even a scratch.

Perfect.

Now it's Warren's turn.

I scramble into the trees behind me and wait.

Seconds later I hear his approach, heralded by squealing brakes and a single syllable repeated over and over and over—"No, no, noooooooo!" and then an "AaaauuUUUUUGGGH!" And with that, Warren is sucking sky.

He's going way too fast. I don't see him take the jump, but I watch him sail through the air as he passes the corner where I'm hiding. He clears the landing strip entirely. His wheels are still several inches above the ground when he rockets straight over the edge of the embankment and into the waiting arms of the trees. He hits them with a crashing, rustling, cracking sound. There might even be crunching. I can't really tell.

I wince.

When all the smashing noises die away, I go over to investigate the damage. Warren is lying in a bloodied heap on a juniper bush at the base of the trees. He's not moving. I scrabble down the cliffside, dirt wedging itself under my fingernails as I try to control my descent. About halfway down, I come across Rico's bike. The front wheel is completely tacoed, bent into the shape of an open clamshell. He's going to be pissed.

Suddenly it hits me. Now that Warren is down, we might all get out of this mess alive.

Might being the operative word. We still have to get away from Deuce. And now we're down a bike too.

I reach for my belt, where I carry my Swiss Army knife. I keep it there, on a ring. There's a whistle attached to it too. My dad trained us early to always keep our knives and whistles right on our bodies in case things went wrong in the bush. I send a silent thanks to Dad for his sensible teachings and general squareness.

When I grab the knife, my hand brushes against the phone inside my pocket. I'd forgotten it was there. I pull it out, yank up the antenna and dial 9-1-1. I hope to god it works out here.

And it does. It takes a minute, but I'm connected with a dispatcher who sounds very far away. I babble on about marijuana and mountain bikes and an armed drug lord on his way to kill us.

"Where are you now?" she asks.

"Um, I don't know," I say. This is a huge problem. "I don't know," I repeat, willing myself not to panic. "We're, um, we're in the North Shore Mountains. We camped near a riverbed last night." I realize I'm not giving her any useful information, but I can't think of what else I can tell her. Should I describe the trees around me?

She solves my problem with a simple question. "Is there anyone I can call who can tell me where you are?"

Relief floods me. I give her the name of the camp.

"Jamie, when I hang up with you, I'm going to call Camp Edgelow to figure out your coordinates," she says. "We're going to send help." She sounds so reassuring. I really want to believe her. "Be very careful," she says. "You are in a dangerous situation."

I almost want to laugh. If only she knew. But instead, I thank her profusely and hang up.

I pull the main blade out from the body of the knife. Pulling off Rico's front tire, I yank out the inner tube. With a quick slice, I cut it in the middle. I use it to tie Warren's hands to a tree trunk. There's a fair amount of extra tubing, so I tie his feet as well. That'll be fun for him when he wakes up.

As I start back up the embankment, I remember the gun. I turn back and feel around on Warren's belt. There it is. I pull it out and stuff it into the back of my shorts. Isn't that where you're supposed to carry a gun? But having a firearm pointing down my shorts makes me feel a bit nervous. I kind of like my butt the way it is, thanks.

I take the gun out and stuff it into the lower pocket of my cargo shorts instead. As I turn and scramble back up the cliffside, a terrible thought hits me. I never asked the dispatcher when help would arrive. In fact, I don't think I even told her when Deuce was supposed to show up.

God. Did I even tell her about Deuce?

As I grab for the phone again, I glance up at the sun. Probably after nine. A sudden shiver jolts me.

I've got less than an hour to get back to the cabin, get everyone loose and get the hell out of this place before this Deuce guy shows up.

I don't have time to make another call.

chapter nineteen

The one bad thing about riding a great stretch of downhill? Yep. What goes down must come up.

I walk Chase's bike past the jump, then slide it into granny gear and get moving. I put one foot in front of the other in a constant forward motion. I don't look up at the trail ahead. It's too discouraging. I just keep spinning. Up, up, up, past the dirt single track and into the grassy deer trail. Up, up, until finally, when my legs are screaming at me to stop, I pop up over the lip of the trail and onto the logging road.

I hammer back along the road toward the cabin. My breath comes ragged in my throat. I'm thirsty again. Already the sun is hot, baking the back of my T-shirt.

I reach the cabin in record time. Damian is still slumped against the tree. I must've hit him good. Maybe he's sleeping off the weed too.

The door to the cabin is still open, the way Warren left it. I can't hear anything from inside. My worry motor starts up again. I drop Chase's bike and climb the stairs. As I do, it strikes me that there might possibly be a third guard that I don't know about. I freeze, terrified by the thought.

But I have to keep moving. I have to try to get the guys out.

I peer around the frame of the door and into the cabin. It's dark as hell in there, but I catch a glimpse of Nolan sitting on the floor next to a table. His arms are behind him. Tied to the table, probably. A slash of duct tape covers his mouth. He sees me peeping in, and his eyes widen. He grunts at me and nods, thumping his feet on the wooden floor. He cranes his head to look around.

Nolan wouldn't be making this much noise if there was another armed thug, I figure, so I step inside. I leave the door open behind me so I can see, but the light only falls a little way inside the cabin. I can't see past the front area.

"You guys okay?" I call. I hear scuffling noises. Someone starts banging. Good. Banging is good. "Okay. You're good now," I say. "It's all good. I'm going to get us out of here."

I take a few steps and squat down by Nolan. "Jesus, Nolan, are you okay?" I peel the tape off his face. His glasses are still there, but they're missing an arm.

He winces as the tape pulls his skin. "I'm okay," he says, after a big gulp of air. "Where are those two idiots?"

Okay, so there *were* only two. That's good.

"I took care of them," I say. It sounds absurd, like a line from a Clint Eastwood movie. But it's true. I did take care of them. "They're tied up, and they won't be getting free anytime soon. What about the others? Is everyone else all right?"

Nolan nods. "I think so. Undo my hands and feet and I can help you get them."

I grab my Swiss Army knife and carefully slice through the duct tape on his ankles. "We've got to move fast, Nolan," I say as I work. "There's another guy called Deuce. He's on his way. I think this is his grow-op. He's coming up to check on things, and he knows we're here. He's probably going to kill us if he finds us."

"How do you know he's on his way?"

"I heard the goons talking on the phone," I reply. "He's planning to be here by ten."

"Ten o'clock?" Nolan squeaks. He looks at his watch. "Jamie, it's, like, nine thirty-five!"

"I know, Nolan," I say. I keep my voice calm. "That's why we have to bust our asses out of here."

"Faster than a rolling O," he agrees. His feet free, Nolan stomps them on the floor to get the circulation moving again.

From deep inside the cabin, the other guys stomp in reply.

"We're coming, guys," Nolan calls. "Jamie's just undoing my hands now."

For once, I appreciate Nolan's tendency to keep people informed. I turn my attention to his hands. "We're down a bike," I say. "Two bikes," I correct myself, remembering that Seth's bike is still in the bushes somewhere. "We've only got three now, for the five of us. We're going to have to double up." I have no idea how that's going to work either. How do you make a quick getaway with someone's butt on your handlebars?

"What about the ATV?" Nolan asks.

Ah, man. The guy's brilliant. I could kiss him. I reach inside my pocket and feel around for the keys. Still there. Perf.

"Good thinking. Yep, we can use that too," I say. I yank off the last of the duct tape. "Okay, let's move. Are there windows in this place? I can't see what I'm doing."

Nolan nods. "I'll see if I can open them."

"If not, there are headlamps in my bag outside," I call after him. I start into the back of the cabin.

"There should be one on the front table," Nolan shouts over his shoulder.

I turn and look. Sure enough, there's a light on the table. I crank it over my helmet and twist it into the ON position. Nolan uncovers a couple of windows and light punches holes in the darkness of the little cabin.

Having the light makes the work go much faster. I can actually look at what I'm doing instead of going mostly by feel.

Within the span of several minutes, Nolan and I have freed everyone. I explain as much as I know about Deuce as we step out into the sunshine. Rico looks like he's been run over by a truck. Chase's easy smile is long gone, replaced by a look of determination. Seth is in full freak-out mode, his eyes rolling around in his head.

"It's nine forty-seven, guys," I say, glancing at Nolan's watch. "We've got to get a move on."

"Let's head 'er," agrees Chase. "If we ride now, we'll be back at the campsite by the time that Deuce guy gets here."

"What if he's got infrared scanners in his helicopter?" asks Nolan suddenly. "If he does, he'll be able to find us in the bushes, no matter where we are. We'd need a bunker to be safe."

This thought scares me. Seth gives off a little moan.

"What makes you so sure he'll come in a chopper?" Rico asks.

"Well," Nolan says, "he's a big-time drug trafficker, right? Do you think a busy guy like that is going to hike in to his grow-op on foot?" He blinks at Rico. "Or maybe he'll ride in on a purple unicorn, Rico." If I wasn't so scared, I'd laugh.

Rico grunts. "Well, still. He might be traveling light. The other guys were on ATVs."

143

Nolan opens his mouth to argue, but nothing comes out. A faraway sound has stolen his words. We all freeze at the same time, eyes locked on each other. Terror rips through us as we listen to the noise that's drawing closer.

It's the sound of a helicopter.

chapter twenty

He's early. I hadn't planned on that. Hadn't even thought about that. Somehow I had convinced myself that Deuce would arrive at the stroke of ten.

And here he is, fifteen minutes ahead of schedule.

"Chase!" I shout. "There's a gun under the porch!" Chase dashes away to grab Damian's gun. I reach for the pistol inside my shorts pocket.

It's gone. I stretch my pocket out and peer inside in disbelief. It must have fallen out when I was biking on that brutal uphill. I've got to go back for the gun!

But as soon as I have that thought, I realize how ridiculous it is. There's no way I'd be able to make it back to the hill, find the gun and get back here to the cabin before Deuce lands his chopper and offs all my friends. I want to scream in frustration, but I force myself to concentrate.

What Rico said might be true—there may be infrared in Deuce's helicopter. Even if we make a run for it, we still might get caught.

We'll have to chance it. There's no other option now. We have one gun. Who knows how many Deuce has? Or how many guys he's bringing with him?

Chase returns with the gun, tucking it into his belt.

"You know how to use that thing?" Nolan shrieks.

Chase raises his eyebrows. "I will when it matters."

The way he says it gives me a shiver. I nod. "Okay. We're going to have to ride. We've only got one gun. Unless anybody saw other weapons in the cabin?" Everyone shakes their heads. "Right. We can't fight. So we run. We have three bikes and an ATV. Who can drive?"

"Hey, man, where's my bike?" asks Rico, looking around.

Chase ignores him. "I'll drive," he says.

"My bike's gone," says Rico. "What happened to it?"

I hold the keys out to Chase. "Your bike is at the bottom of a very steep cliff," I tell Rico. "In very bad shape."

Rico looks like I've stabbed him in the stomach. "What? How did that happen?" he asks.

"Rico!" Nolan shrills. "This is not the time to discuss the finer points of what happened to your bike! This is a time to get the hell away from an armed criminal in a helicopter who will shoot us all in the head and throw us down the mountainside if we don't get out of here right bloody NOW!"

147

Seth bursts out laughing. Within seconds, his laughter unravels into hysterical giggles. He's starting to lose it. We're all starting to lose it. We've got to get out of here.

Chase recognizes this too. "Time to move, boys," he says. "You're coming with me, Rico. Seth, Jamie, Nolan, you're riding. Climb on. Let's roll."

Muttering about his mangled bike, Rico climbs onto the ATV. Chase fires it up. Everyone else moves to grab a bike.

"Uh, guys?" Nolan says. "My bike doesn't have a seat."

Seth starts giggling again.

"Right. Hang on," I say. I race across the expanse of grass in front of the cabin. An expanse of grass that's perfect for landing a helicopter, I realize with a queasy shudder. I snatch the seat up from where I left it after clonking Damian.

I sprint back to Nolan. "Here." Breathless, I wiggle the seat onto the post. My fingers fly as I push down the quick-release clamp. Nolan climbs on.

"We'll bring up the rear," Chase adds. "You guys go."

I look at Chase. "You sure?" The noise from the helicopter is getting louder. It's not far now. Rico's face is stony.

Chase nods and pats the gun on his hip. "No worries. I got your back. Seth, you're in the lead. Take us out of here," Chase says. It's good thinking on Chase's part, I realize. He knows he's got to bring Seth back down to earth. Putting him in the lead gives him something to hold on to.

We swing up and hammer. Seth leads, and I bring up the rear. Nolan rides between us. Chase and Rico buzz along behind. The helicopter drowns out the noise from the ATV's engine.

Suddenly, a strong wind grabs the trees and whips them around in a frenzied dance. Dust and bits of twigs rise up off the path. Soon we're choking.

"Go, go!" I scream from the back of the line. Somehow, we speed up.

The chopper is almost upon us. With an ear-splitting roar, its top rises into view off the berm to our left. No one looks over. We just concentrate on getting the hell out of sight. Up ahead, the double track curves away and our path dives into the trees. If he spots us heading into the forest, Deuce will know where we've gone, but at least we'll be under the cover of the trees.

But if we can make it into the trees first—and if he doesn't have heat-seeking technology onboard—there's a chance he'll never find us.

Ahead of me, Seth slows down. What the hell is he thinking? This isn't the time to be putting on the brakes. "Speed it up, Seth!" I screech from my place at the rear.

He shouts something back at me, but it's lost in the roar of wind and rotors and motors. Then, suddenly, we're stopping.

I slam on my brakes. Yanking my handle-bars to the right, I clip Nolan's back end. Nolan is pushed forward and plows into Seth. I fly off my bike, landing with a grunt in the soft grass.

Behind me, Chase moves quickly, veering the ATV in the opposite direction.

He slows it to a controlled stop off the path to the left.

"What the—?" I hear him say.

"What are you *doing*, Seth?" I shout as I spring to my feet. "We're trying to get *away* from the freakin' helicopter, or haven't you noticed?"

But Seth doesn't answer me. He's standing astride his bike. He can't go any farther, I see now, because his way is blocked.

By an ATV.

With Mitch on it.

What the hell is going on?

chapter twenty-one

It takes me a moment to realize that the noise from the helicopter is fading. My brain clanks and squeals a bit as it processes this information. We haven't been shot. The chopper is moving away from where we're standing.

That means Deuce hasn't spotted us.

Then Mitch pulls out a gun. And suddenly I understand.

Deuce has indeed spotted us.

He's standing right in front of us.

Nolan's the first to put it into words. "Oh my god," he whispers. "*You're* Deuce?"

Mitch ignores Nolan's question. Asks one of his own. "You guys headed somewhere?" His face is deadly cold. So different from yesterday, when he was all smiles.

As he speaks, Mitch brings the gun up so it's pointing at Seth. My heart stops, and the blood drains from my head. Blackness closes in on the edge of my vision.

He's got a gun on my baby brother.

I swallow. "Mitch," I say. My voice sounds like it's coming from a mile away. Deep and slow, like I'm in a dream. I take a deep breath. *Breathe.*

I have to stall. Figure out a way to get the gun away from Mitch. I curse the fact that I dropped Warren's gun on the hill. Even though I don't have a clue how to shoot it, I'd feel about a thousand percent better if I had it in my hand.

Where's Chase? He's got a gun. I look around, but I can't see him. Rico's here. But where the hell is Chase?

"Mitch," I say again. Mitch looks at me when I speak, but he keeps the gun trained on Seth. He motions for Seth to come and stand beside him. Seth drops his bike and does what he's asked. His blue eyes goggle out from his white face as he looks to me for help.

I'm trying my best, Seth, I think. I don't know if I can figure this one out.

"Looks like you kiddies got in over your heads, eh?" Mitch asks. His voice is cold. "Went snooping where you weren't supposed to."

Nolan speaks. "We won't tell anyone, Mitch. I promise. We swear. This can be our secret." He looks around at us. "Right, guys?" Like robots, we all nod.

Mitch laughs. It's a scary noise, dry and scratchy. Suddenly he stops laughing and turns his cool eyes on Nolan. "Too late for bargaining, little guy. You've seen too much already." Mitch moves his thumb, and the gun makes a little *click*. The blackness swims around my vision again. The sound of the safety popping off is just like it is in the movies.

Except this is no movie.

This is real.

"Wait," Rico breaks in. "If you're Deuce, then...who was that in the helicopter?"

"That was the cops," says Mitch calmly. I see Seth's lips part a little bit at these words. He draws in a deep breath and closes his eyes. My own heart does a little double-skip at the thought that the police are nearby. They must have landed the chopper back at the cabin.

"I'm thinking it was one of you wise guys that called them," Mitch continues. "Doesn't matter who, because, see, here's how it is," he says, reaching inside his jacket. "None of you are gonna be talking to anyone about this. Ever." He pulls out a long black cylinder. Screws it on to the end of his 9mm.

A silencer. This is insane.

Mitch continues calmly. "I'm going to march your stupid, snoopy little asses far into the forest and waste you all before the cops figure out what happened."

I need to buy time to let the police find us here. I have to keep Mitch talking.

Suddenly I see Chase pop out of the trees behind Mitch. I hope to god no one's face gives him away. I steal a quick glance at Nolan, but he's holding it together. Seth's facing toward us, which is good, because he wouldn't be able to keep his head on straight. Chase gives me a thumbs-up. I raise my chin slightly in return.

I trust that Chase has a plan, so I just focus on my job. Keep Mitch here for a couple minutes longer. "Mitch, look," I say. "We won't say anything about this. Why don't you just...head right back the way you came, and let's forget this whole thing happened. We won't tell the cops anything about you, okay?"

"Yeah," Nolan chimes in. "We don't want to see you in jail, man. The whole racing scene would starve." Nolan's pretty good at sounding cool under pressure.

Mitch laughs again. "Stop trying to stall, guys. It's game over. Now move." He waves me, Rico and Nolan over with his gun.

Mitch's eyes narrow as he counts us. "Where the hell is Chase?"

Before Mitch can turn to look for him, Chase arcs his bike pump across Mitch's body. Toward the hand that's holding the gun. The pump makes solid contact with the back of Mitch's hand.

CRACK!

Mitch screams and drops the gun. Lightning fast, he reaches back with his other hand to grab Chase.

I don't wait to see what happens next. I take a running leap and tackle Mitch, pinning him to the ground. And then, like a dam suddenly opening, everyone's on him, grabbing arms and legs and feet and hands.

In a few short seconds, we've got Mitch flipped over on his stomach. Rico sits on his feet while Chase holds his hands behind his back. Seth tears off a piece of duct tape to wrap his wrists.

Nolan shakes his head sadly. "Looks like it's your unlucky day, Mitch," he says.

Seth slaps the piece of duct tape across Mitch's mouth as he starts to protest. He holds the roll of tape out to me. His hand trembles slightly. "Care to do the honors, Jamie?"

"No, thanks," I say. "I've had more than my fair share of tying guys up this morning. Knock yourself out, little brother."

But Seth doesn't get the chance.

Behind us, a police dog barks. The officer leading the dog spots us and lifts a radio to his mouth. He speaks briefly and then breaks into a jog in our direction. "You guys okay?" he calls.

When he's confirmed that we're all in one piece, he surveys the scene. "Looks like you've managed to get things under control by yourselves," he says with a note of admiration.

"Yup. We've snagged a nice criminal here for you, officer," says Nolan. "Name's Mitch Woodgrove."

"We came looking for a guy called Deuce," says the cop. "Isn't Mitch Woodgrove a famous mountain biker?"

Seth nods. "He is." He points to Mitch, who's still pinned under Chase and Rico. "That's your Deuce."

A flicker of surprise registers on the cop's face, and then he's all business again. He speaks into his radio again, briefly, then turns to Chase. "Are you the one who called for help?" he asks.

"No, that was our brave man Jamie," says Chase. He nods in my direction.

"Got a minute?" the cop asks me.

I nod. We walk a few steps away, and he writes in a notepad as I tell him everything I know, from start to finish. Stumbling on the grow-op. Nolan and Rico going missing. The dead sat phone. Seth being taken. My immobilizing Warren and Damian. Us realizing Mitch was Deuce. Taking him down.

As I talk, I watch them cart Mitch away in handcuffs. He shoots me a bitter glare. I can't help but shudder.

I sketch the cop a rough map of where I've left Warren in the trees. By the time I'm done giving him my statement, I'm thirsty as hell. The officer thanks me and tells me I can go join the others. I look around.

A couple of cops have begun chopping down the stalks of weed with machetes. They've got a lot of work ahead of them. Another one drifts around the property, taking photos and writing notes. Turns out Mitch runs a bunch of these grow-ops. Or he used to, anyway. The police have been shutting them down as they find them, but they've never been able to get their hands on the guy.

Until today.

I join the others where they're sitting. A police officer has already taken statements from them too and left them with some food. Granola bars, protein bars, dried fruit, beef jerky, cheese and chocolate bars. Sweet. Famished, I dive in. We pass around a couple of bottles of Gatorade.

"Well, at least they've finally caught Deuce," says Nolan. "He'll probably get twenty-five years."

"At least," agrees Rico.

"I just can't believe that Mitch is Deuce," says Chase, shaking his head. "I thought he was such a great guy." We all nod.

"Holy hell, what a day for you, eh, Jamie?" says Rico.

I nod. "Definitely a death march," I say. "Glad it's over now."

Chase punches my shoulder. "You rock, J. We'd all be dead if it wasn't for you, you know that?" Everyone nods.

"Back at you," I say to him. "That was a pretty nice piece of hand-smashing you pulled there at the end."

"You know," says Seth, chewing on a piece of beef jerky, "if I didn't know any better, I'd have to say my big brother is a hero."

He holds his fist out to me. I grin and bump.

"Hear, hear," says Nolan, and breaks into applause.

While everyone is still clapping, Seth leans forward. "You know, you've always been my hero," he says. He looks away. "You stupid jerk."

"Yeah? Well," I say, lowering my voice and looking straight into his sky-blue eyes. "You've always been a stupid jerk."

We both laugh.

Acknowledgments

I'd like to thank Sarah Harvey for helping me make this manuscript better with each revision. Thanks, too, to Andrew Wooldridge, who opened the door in the first place, and to the amazing, lovable and hardworking staff at Orca. You're magic, every one of you.

Alex Van Tol grew up reading a wide range of books, from Enid Blyton to Stephen King. She has worked with kids all her life as a swim instructor, camp counselor, teacher and mother. She traded the chalkboard for the keyboard in 2007. Alex's first novel with Orca Book Publishers was *Knifepoint*. She lives and writes (but no longer mountain bikes) in Victoria, British Columbia.

ALSO AVAILABLE BY
ALEX VAN TOL

978-1-55469-411-2 pb
978-1-55469-412-9 lib

MIKE HAS FALLEN FOR HIS BEST FRIEND, Lindsay. And he's pretty sure she feels the same way, until a simple misunderstanding destroys Lindsay's trust.

When Lindsay ends up in a compromising situation, someone is filming the whole thing, and the footage goes viral. Mike has to help Lindsay in her time of greatest need.

Available in English and Spanish

KNIFEPOINT

978-1-55469-305-4 pb
978-1-55469-306-1 lib

ALEX VAN TOL

A PUNTA DE CUCHILLO

ALEX VAN TOL

978-1-55469-863-9 pb

JILL TOOK A JOB THAT SOUNDED PERFECT

for the summer, guiding tourists on trail rides in the beautiful mountains. She didn't realize that the money was terrible, the hours long and the co-workers insufferable. After a blowup with her boss, she takes a lone man into the mountains for a ride, only to find that he is a dangerous killer. When Jill fights back and manages to escape, she is in a desperate race to survive and make it to safety.

Titles in the Series

orca sports

orca sports

For more information on all the books
in the Orca Sports series, please visit
www.orcabook.com.